Monstrous Alterations

Monstrous Alterations

STORIES BY CHRISTOPHER BARZAK

LETHE PRESS

MONSTROUS ALTERATIONS

Stories by CHRISTOPHER BARZAK

FOR

RICHARD BOWES,

Whose voice is always beside me.

"Everything you love will probably be lost,
but in the end, love will return in another way."

FRANZ KAFKA

CONTENTS

Introduction: *On the Art of Alteration*   1

Sister Twelve: Confessions of a Party Monster   13

For the Applause of Shadows   31

Eat Me, Drink Me, Love Me   51

The Trampling   69

The Creeping Women   83

Invisible Men   107

Dorothy, Rising   132

The Boy Who Grew Up   143

The 24 Hour Brother   161

Kafka's Circus   171

Story Notes   189

ON THE ART
OF ALTERATION

OUR LIVES ARE POPULATED WITH stories we've heard, seen, or read five, ten, fifteen—a thousand—times already, and sometimes these stories return to us in a different guise than the one we remember. Some stories become films, plays, musicals, or graphic novels. Some are even turned into toy and clothing franchises. Stories can be transfigured in so many ways beyond the format of their original presentation. Stories can be uprooted, transplanted, pruned into a different shape, thrown into a blender with other stories, or strained through the filter of a new perception. With just a few striking alterations, what we once thought we knew through and through becomes something strange and unfamiliar.

The first time I came across Angela Carter's collection, *The Bloody Chamber*, in which the fairy tales of the Grimm Brothers, Charles Perrault, and Hans Christian Anderson have been filtered through the feminist perspective that Carter turned upon any subject matter she handled, and in which the stories have also been restyled in a florid, hothouse language,

I was stunned. Prior to encountering her stories back in my early twenties, I'd only thought of adaptation as the sort of thing where Disney took old fairy tales and, in the typical Disney family-friendly manner, rinsed them of all the mud and muck they'd acquired throughout the passage of time. And maybe if those writers involved in adapting the old stories were feeling adventurous, a change in point of view character might be the most extreme alteration made. A feared witch could now become the heroine, for instance. It was a safe and winning choice, in terms of pleasing both the happy-ending crowd as well as those enlightenment-oriented audiences who prefer a good moral to be delivered.

Carter's retold fairy tales were something else—something I'd not really seen before—and they awakened a desire in me to write stories that were in conscious conversation with the stories of others, stories that had obsessed me to the point of driving me to want to write fiction in the first place. I didn't know how to do this. I only knew that I wanted to figure out a way.

My earliest attempts at writing in this way were not complicated revisions or adaptations of a prior text. More often than not, my early stories were ones that simply wore their influences on their sleeves, that made references to predecessor texts in some way. The first story I ever published, in fact, was one of these referential sorts of stories. It was about a troubled young woman who returns home for her mother's funeral and melts down as she confronts the idea that she'll never be able to make amends with her mother now that she's dead. I titled it "A Mad Tea Party" and called the protagonist Alice, decorating the scenes with allusions and imagistic references to Lewis Carroll's *Alice in Wonderland*. A porcelain cat destroyed after it's been knocked off a shelf seems to grin in Cheshire fashion. Tears fall in what *feels* like a flood, filling the room my Alice sits in, grieving, until the walls around her seem as though they might fly apart like a house of cards. I transplanted images that had mostly been fantastical and strange in Carroll's famous book into a domestic tale of grief as a way to describe my Alice's interior world, which is in chaos as she collapses under the weight of regret.

When I wrote that story, I was young—twenty-two—and I was still working very intuitively. It didn't occur to me until later, when I became a more conscious and practiced writer, that I really couldn't call what I'd done in that story something so simple as literary allusion. The story I wrote could have been written without *Alice in Wonderland* acting as a shadow story informing all of the mostly domestic events I described, and it would have been a much different story without those Wonderland references. It would most likely have been incredibly mundane, overly familiar, a typical story of grief that we've encountered many times. Without asking readers to move back and forth between my story and Carroll's as they read, it would have been a less playful and complicated reading experience.

Another story of this type that I wrote occurred a couple of years after that Wonderland-referencing story. I wrote it during a period when I found myself trying to break away from a relationship that was wrong for me, the kind where the person I loved seemed incapable of loving me without also causing a lot of pain. I didn't know how to articulate the experience, and the inability to articulate that kind of pain felt suffocating. It was only after I began to work through it by way of the imagery and archetypes of a particular fairy tale that I found my voice—or at least *a* voice—to speak from. Finding that voice was something I needed to remedy my frustration with feeling silenced. I called the story "The Cure" because of that and, small as it may be, I will offer it here, placed within this essay as an Easter egg:

THE CURE

WHEN MY HEART WAS BREAKING, I went to my grandmother and said, "Grandmother, my heart is breaking over and over. My insides are like broken glass. Tell me how to cure this pain."

Grandmother leaned on her gnarled crook. She tapped it against the floor and said, "Your heart, dear girl, cannot break over and over. It breaks once. What you feel afterwards is the memory of its breaking. A broken heart cannot be healed."

Unsatisfied with her answer, I said, "Grandmother, you have healed other hearts. Why not mine?"

"Enough," she said, and struggled up from her recliner, pulling her red shawl tighter. She waved me into the kitchen. On her stove, a pot boiled with something vinegary. "Sit," said Grandmother, and I sat at the Formica table patterned with red and white roses. Grandmother ladled the liquid out of the pot and peered at me over her shoulder. "You have always been weak, girl. Are you sure about this?"

"Yes," I nodded. "Take it out of me, whatever it is. Make me *me* again."

"As I suspected," she said. "You are one that he eats from the inside, rather than devouring you whole."

"Yes," I said, remembering how he slid down inside me, and how at first I thought him special — a beast, but honest and noble.

"This is my special recipe." She shuffled over to the table with the ladle steaming. The liquid slopped over the sides of the ladle, hissing against the linoleum. "But be warned. To heal can be as painful as hurting."

"Anything," I said.

She grinned. "You are a child of my bloodline. He hasn't ridden you too far, so far. Now open wide." She lifted the ladle to my lips and poured.

The liquid went down scalding. I almost screamed, but as I started, Grandmother punched me in the stomach. "Out!" she shouted. "You have no power over her!"

She continued punching until I began choking. He was coming up fast. My throat bulged with him. A moment later, his claws unhinged my jaws to exit, and he pushed himself through my mouth. Grandmother lifted her crook as he slipped in the slop on the floor. She cracked his backside. He howled. She struck him once more. "Out!" she bellowed, and he ran through the door, a flash of fur and feral madness.

I slouched in the chair and held my mouth together, crying. Grandmother asked if it was worth it. I nodded.

Anything, I had said, and I had meant it.

"I'm sorry," she said, stroking my forehead with a towel, wiping the blood from my mouth. "In the old times," she said, "this was easier. We used an ax to open up the people he'd crawled into, but they never survived. This is the best," she said, placing her cheek against mine. "The best I can offer."

I groaned, and she nodded in sympathy. "A piece of advice, though," she said. "Next time, dear, love carefully. Stay on the path."

From the outside, the story looks like a clearly conscious reworking of Little Red Riding Hood, but while I wrote it felt more like the images and archetypes of that old tale were working *through* me rather than me reworking the images and archetypes. The direction of the writing was, in a way, the reverse of what I now think of as retellings. The story and its symbols were available for me to use for my own purposes, which happened to be personal, but I hadn't been consciously trying to do this. I was simply casting about for a way to work through my own emotional experience, and these symbols and images from a fairy tale told hundreds of years ago and transferred to me through a variety of mediums since childhood, made themselves available to me to make sense of something in my life.

Some years later, after writing many more stories, after writing my first novel, after I'd continued swimming more into the deep end of my subconscious as a writer rather than making laps across the surface, I found myself coming up for air as I read this passage from Jonathan Lethem's essay, "The Ecstasy of Influence":

"Most artists are brought to their vocation when their own nascent gifts are awakened by the work of a master. That is to say, most artists are converted to art by art itself. Finding one's voice isn't just an emptying and purifying oneself of the words of others but an adopting and embracing of filiations, communities, and discourses. Inspiration could be called inhaling the memory of an act never experienced. Invention, it must be humbly admitted, does not consist in creating out of void but out of chaos. Any artist knows these truths, no matter how deeply he or she submerges that knowing."

I can distinctly remember how, before I'd even finished reading the last sentence of that paragraph, I felt something stir inside me. Maybe the truths I'd submerged, as Lethem describes them. The truths that my own writing, that my own voice, had been forged out of other voices. The truth that I—as well as the stories I told—was a part of something bigger. Something much more communal than the image or myth of the writer or artist as a supreme and sole originator allows.

It wasn't quite what I'd call a shocking realization, but it was one that continued to affect me for a long time after, forcing me to move further out of my more regular realm of intuition and further into the realm of awareness, though not always in a constant or consistent progress. These submerged truths, truths that had not been fully recognized, flickered to life in an almost animated fashion, flaring brightly sometimes, going dark again at others.

The light that epiphany brings doesn't always remain a permanent feature in our mental landscapes. Sometimes we have to relearn knowledge until it becomes firmly rooted in us. Once this particular knowledge eventually took root, I found myself turning back to Angela Carter's *The Bloody Chamber*, rereading her revisionist fairy tales with a greater pleasure than I did the first time I encountered them a decade earlier. And while revisiting them, I remembered how they'd once sparked a desire in me to write stories in conversation with the stories of others. By the time I turned the last page of the last story, I found myself wanting to further the desire I'd first felt as a twenty-two year old, and soon after I began to write a story that retells part of H.G. Wells' short novel, *The Invisible Man*, from the point of view of the young maid in the inn where the Invisible Man takes refuge for several months as he attempts to create a potion that will make him visible again.

It was my first attempt to consciously rework a story by another author beyond mere reference, and I chose it as my first attempt because I had a somewhat bristly relationship with that novel. As a teenager, I'd read *The Invisible Man* and loved it, but with one particular reservation: Wells had rendered the rural characters in his book mostly as caricatures and stereotypes, making easy jokes of their habits and manners and ways of speaking. As an adult reader, with a greater critical awareness, all of this bothered me to no end. Probably because I'd grown up in a rural town, I was sensitive to unfair depictions of rural people. Probably because I'd grown up in a working-class family, I was sensitive to unfair depictions of working-class people. In Wells' story, I was annoyed by how the character Millie, a sixteen-year-old girl living and working at the inn where the Invisible Man takes up residence, was mainly treated as comic relief. Largely by way of her manner of speech, which is rough and uneducated, Wells probably got easy laughs out of his readers whenever Millie entered a scene. So, as I began to consider a revision of this story that might right what I perceived to be an unnecessary wrong in the original, I knew that I wanted to give Millie a voice in which the depth of her humanity and intelligence could be seen and acknowledged by readers.

I began to write by retelling the strange events Millie had witnessed at the inn from her point of view, in a first-person voice I created by way of using actual lines of dialogue Wells wrote for her, and then by devouring a dictionary entirely devoted to the slang of the West Sussex region of England during the time period in which *The Invisible Man* takes place.

This was a lot of work, and it was a much different creative process from how I'd written anything before. It forced me to change and grow as a writer in ways that felt fresh and strangely liberating. One time was all it took. Before I'd even finished that retelling, I was addicted. And soon after, I began to write a retelling of Poe's "William Wilson" using a different point of view, with a different explanation for the untimely (or timely, depending on your perspective) appearances of the doppelganger that haunts the cruel William Wilson in Poe's original.

It went on like this over a period of several years: me rethinking stories I loved but with which I'd had issues of various kinds. Political, aesthetic, personal. In the end, I wrote a sheaf of stories of this transformative type. Retellings. Adaptations. Remixes. Altered narrative art. There are a lot of different terms to refer to this kind of approach to storytelling, and each one carries with it a different nuance. I experimented with as many different ways to approach the art of alteration as I could think of in that period of time. And in the process of experimenting, I identified six particular theories (or strategies) for retellings that I pursued most often, in different combinations, as follows:

RETELLING AS A MATTER OF EMPHASIS: This kind of retelling revises the original narrative to bring greater emphasis to some aspect or theme that was perhaps only hinted at in the original, or that might have even been entirely absent. Some of Angela Carter's revisionist fairy tales, for example, adhere to the original plots of their prototypes, but those plots are funneled through Carter's feminist sensibility, which layers new meaning to the plots, in effect interpreting the plots of the originals to emphasize the themes and dynamics of gender, sexuality, and power.

RETELLING AS A MATTER OF PERSPECTIVE: Perhaps the most popular or familiar sort of retellings are those that exchange the original point of view character for a new perspective. These are the sorts of retellings and adaptations that often make their way into film adaptations. Disney, for instance, took its own film retelling of "Sleeping Beauty" and then altered it a second time in the film *Maleficent*, from the point of view of the witch who curses Beauty to sleep forever. In the original version, the perspective belongs to Beauty and her royal family, and through that view the witch is seen as a great evil. In *Maleficent*, however, told from the witch's perspective, we learn that Beauty's father was once the witch's childhood love, and we learn of his betrayal due to his grasping for power within the kingdom. This motivates Maleficent's desire for vengeance and recasts the story so that she is no longer simply an evil entity, but a vulnerable and sympathetic character.

RETELLING AS A MATTER OF TIME AND PLACE: Another favorite of filmmakers who adapt the stories of others to their own ends. Re-decorating might be a more appropriate term for this sort of retelling, since it's the kind where a writer takes an old tale and dresses it up in new furnishings, usually by way of contextualizing the story within a different time and place from the original. The original plot is often retained, the characters (or at least the character types) are usually retained, but the setting—the time and place—is altered. This can often make an old story feel new, and it can often serve as critical commentary about the new time and place into which the old tale has been transplanted. The 1988 film, *Scrooged*, for instance, recasts Charles Dickens' *A Christmas Carol* in the world of a late 80s TV executive. The movie, *Bridget Jones's Diary*, recontextualizes the plot of Jane Austen's *Pride and Prejudice* for a more modern turn-of-the-twentieth-century England, comparing and contrasting how much (or how little) had changed in the romantic and social lives of Londoners of various class backgrounds since Austen's time.

RETELLING AS A MATTER OF LANGUAGE: Angela Carter is again perhaps the best example for this sort of approach. In *The Bloody Chamber*, using lush and lyrical language, she exacts a stylistic transformation on fairy tales that, in their older, original forms, were mostly told in a plain prose with few flourishes. Even if Carter hadn't brought new meaning to the original stories filtered through the emphasis of a modern feminist perspective, the florid language she used for these retellings would have made something old feel very new in the aesthetic experience (and if not new, then at least very different).

REMIXES: Of course there are retellings and adaptations that use more than one of these approaches at the same time, and there is also a kind of retelling that I think of more as remixes, which may work with multiple original story sources to create a kind of mosaic or multi-layered retelling. Kelly Link is a writer who occasionally reworks the materials of fairy tales in this way. Her story "Travels With The Snow Queen" is an exemplary model of this sort, where she mainly explores the old Hans Christian Anderson tale, but because of the narrative point of view—a whimsical second person narrator who runs a fairy tale tourism company—references to Cinderella, the Little Mermaid, the Goose Girl, and other fairy tales are made, creating something more than just a plot retelling (though that occurs as well), or a modernized version of the original story. Link does something that feels more like the way music is remixed, where multiple songs are combined, a beat from one, a refrain from another, converging and diverging, blending together, until something entirely different from any of the individual sources emerges.

TRANSFORMATIONS: And, of course, there are those stories that owe a great deal to an original narrative without leaving a lot of breadcrumbs along the path they took through the forest as they wandered further from home and entered into foreign territory. These kinds of stories have been transformed in ways that may not allow a reader to immediately recognize where they've come from. These stories have lost their accents, bought new clothes, changed their names, invented new identities, like Holly Golightly, ever reinventing herself in Truman Capote's *Breakfast at Tiffany's*. They seem familiar, but there's something about them you can't put your finger on. Their core concept may be similar to another story you've read, but the author has filed off the serial numbers, changed the names, relocated the setting, displaced the time period, or even reversed the original concept so that the resulting story is a negative image of the original. Someone widely read and in possession of a good memory can sometimes sniff these types of transformed stories out. I've included only one of these types in this collection. "The 24 Hour Brother" is my spin on "The Curious Case of Benjamin Button" where you won't find any of F. Scott Fitzgerald's original characters living and breathing. Nor will you find the style of his telling, nor the time period in which the original story was set. The one thing several reviewers of this transformed story noticed in its original magazine appearance was how it reminded them of the Benjamin Button story despite no obvious relationship to it. It is both homage to the original as well as a critical reversal of the original story's concept.

❧

OTHER APPROACHES AND TECHNIQUES FOR retelling and transforming narratives originated by others exist. These are just some of the routes I took as I altered stories (and a poem, in one case) for my own purposes.

Purpose. What is the purpose of retelling or altering stories of the past, anyway? Why isn't all art original? The myth of the artist who originates story from within a vacuum is a powerful illusion rooted in the hyper-individualism of western thought. But the artist who retells, translating from one language to another, one culture to another, or one time period to another, has traditionally served a universal literary purpose, and will continue to do so, as long as a civilization desires to retain a thread of continuity: to weave the past into the present, and the present into the future. To bind together, to restore, to carry forth what might otherwise be lost, to alter something that has lost its function over the grinding span of time in order to make it work again.

Retellings can revive stories that might otherwise have been buried beneath the rubble of the past. These stories are carried beyond the mortal life of their authors into the future, passed on like candles in a dark corridor, their light breaking through the shadows into the present, their meaning sometimes changed as the world changes.

Retellings can reveal the evolution—the progress or decline—of a culture by contrasting the differences between their contemporary renderings with those of their past.

For me, though, the purpose of retelling stories—the purpose of retelling these stories in particular—is to participate actively in the communal storytelling impulse that many years ago pulled me into an activity done mostly in solitude: writing. An activity that somehow, despite its inherent solitude, has brought me further into the congress of the world.

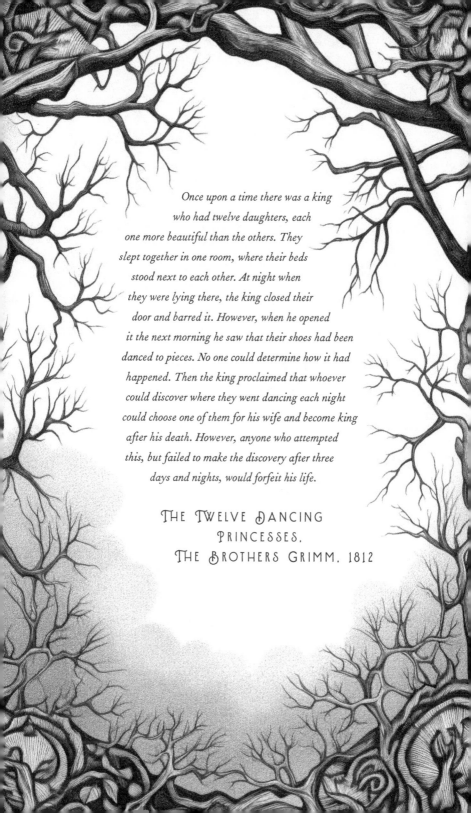

Once upon a time there was a king
who had twelve daughters, each
one more beautiful than the others. They
slept together in one room, where their beds
stood next to each other. At night when
they were lying there, the king closed their
door and barred it. However, when he opened
it the next morning he saw that their shoes had been
danced to pieces. No one could determine how it had
happened. Then the king proclaimed that whoever
could discover where they went dancing each night
could choose one of them for his wife and become king
after his death. However, anyone who attempted
this, but failed to make the discovery after three
days and nights, would forfeit his life.

THE TWELVE DANCING
PRINCESSES.
THE BROTHERS GRIMM. 1812

S I S T E R
T W E L V E :

C O N F E S S I O N S   O F   A
P A R T Y   M O N S T E R

IT DIDN'T TAKE WITH ME, the world and its rules, the things it expected of me. In the end, that's the only reason why I find myself still here after all these countless years, and still I refuse to leave the scene. If you drop a beat, I'm on it. If I hear the slightest scratch, I'm ready to spin. If my shoes give out, if I split a sole or break a heel, it doesn't matter. I kick them off and keep on dancing like the music and my body can't be put on pause.

We have a date—the music, the dance floor, and I. We're going to move all night long if we have anything to say about it.

If I gave a damn about the world, though, and what it wanted from me, I'd be sitting in a high-backed chair right now with my needlepoint in my lap, collecting a fine layer of dust as I concentrated on a difficult stitch. My father liked seeing us girls do things like that. "Nothing more beautiful than to see a young lady with her head bent over a hoop," he used to say as he passed through our room, where my sisters would be sitting in that exact position. Then he'd notice me heaped in the corner chair, where I'd pulled my legs under me and sat hunched over the yellowed pages of a novel, and he would *tsk*. Seriously, he would *tsk*. Once, he told me, "You are quite fortunate to have been born last of all my daughters."

"Why is that?" I asked, placing my finger upon the sentence I was just then reading before looking up into his disappointed face, eyes blinking beneath their furry salt and pepper mantle. The gold crown on his head was tilted a little to the side, as if a beggar or a drunkard had just accosted him.

"Because the youngest child always gets away with more than his or her older siblings," was his answer. Then he turned to walk away.

"Is that luck, Father," I asked, "or is it just the intelligent observation of others going through life experiences before you have, and then analyzing the results of their conclusions, that leads to smarter decision-making?"

"Tsk-tsk," said my father. Looking over his shoulder, he shook his head as if I were a bitter pill his advisor forced him to swallow each night for the sake of his health.

THE YOUNGEST CHILD IS ALSO supposedly the one everyone likes (except the older siblings, of course, because they tend to feel jealous of all the attention diverted to the baby). But whether any of that is true or just psychoanalytical bullshit doesn't really matter. What matters is that, somehow, that psychoanalytical bullshit sometimes maps on to your life in a real way; and at those times, if you're a person who's able to be honest with yourself, you have to sit around and think, *Well, okay, maybe I should pay attention to what this is telling me?*

In my case, yes, almost everyone liked me, except for my sisters, who I always felt either hated or thought little of me, because of both my prolonged innocence and also because of the way I often stupidly pointed out the flaws in their thinking without realizing how embarrassing that might be for them. Really, my pointing out their flaws was a symptom of my innocence—back then I thought it was a *good* thing to be honest with people, no matter what—but that explanation doesn't excuse the hurt I must have caused them. In the end, what matters is that I too often told the truth as if it were as ordinary as the air we breathe, and because of that I could sometimes make my sisters feel like the lowest creatures in existence.

"I told you so." Those were the words I often found myself using with my sisters in the year after my brother-in-law, the soldier who I'm sure has gone on by now to be king in place of my father, discovered our secret. "I told you so, I told you so," I would tell my sisters in the eleven months that passed during the year after that man brought a halt to our dancing.

I said this so often because I so often realized things that my sisters never noticed, and they always made me feel like a stupid little girl when I said things like, "Shouldn't we wait to leave until we hear the guard snoring?" or "Shouldn't we maybe tie him to his chair anyway, just in case he's fooling? That way, he can't follow us down into the clubs."

They laughed at me, my sisters. They said, "Oh child, you are always so afraid." But I wasn't afraid. I was never afraid. I was just observant and cautious. I knew that soldier had something on us, I just didn't know what.

Turns out, he had a cloak that could make him invisible, and he had some wisdom from an old crone he'd met in the woods on his way to our castle to solve the secret of our nightly disappearances for our father. The wisdom the old crone gave him was this: *Don't drink the cup of wine they'll give you at the end of the night, but make them think that you did.*

It was good advice, really. Old crones know a lot. They've seen shit go down that most young people only hear about in songs and movies. The wine that we gave to our nightly guards, to our would-be-saviors and suitors, was always drugged. It put them dead asleep within minutes of sipping it twice, and while they were nodding off in the corner, their minds growing black as a bog, my sisters and I—well, the twelve of us would go out dancing.

❧

IT STARTED WHEN I WAS sixteen, us all going out in the middle of the night like that, coming home in the wee hours of the morning with our shoes completely in tatters. It started after my oldest sister found the secret passage beneath her bed, while she was looking for an earring she'd dropped as she undressed from a particularly dreadful ball that evening. My father was trying to marry her off that year, as at twenty-eight Sister One was far beyond the age by which most princesses would have already got hitched. Sister One didn't really want to get married, though. She had nightmares about diamond rings and multi-tiered white cakes, and some mornings she'd wake up screaming. But she endured my father's matchmaking because she had to. She was a dutiful princess, Sister One, even if she hated her duties.

So we were all back in our room, exhausted after a night of "Pleased to make your acquaintance, I'm sure," and glad-handing every major royal who-de-who and every minor foreign ambassador my father introduced us to, when my oldest sister dropped her left earring and knelt down to look beneath her bed for it, only to alarm the rest of us when she said, "What's *this*?" as if she'd found something either terrible or else terribly exciting. All of us stopped fiddling with our laces to look over our shoulders at her where she was crouched on the floor, her head stuffed under the bed. "What's this then?" Sister One said again, and she scurried under the bed like a common rodent.

She came out a few seconds later, gasping for air like she'd just come up from swimming underwater, and begged us to help her push the bed aside. None of us knew what was going on, but we were sisters—we did things for each other when one of us asked a favor—so we lined up on one side of the bed, all twelve of us, and gave it a good shove.

All of us gasped, too, when we stepped back and saw the glowing silver outline of a door etched into the flagstones before us. "Look here," Sister One said, and she put her hand upon the center of the outlined door. The floor began to shift, stone grinding on stone, and seemed to lower a little. Sister One looked up with a wicked grin cutting across her face; then she looked down and put her hand on the center of the stone door again, making it grind ever so dully as it moved lower and lower, until we could see nothing but a few of the top steps of a staircase leading down into thick darkness.

"What is it?" one of my other sisters asked.

And Sister One said, "A secret passage, clearly!"

Just then, a soft sound flowed out of the passageway, like dandelion seeds blown upon a current.

"What's that?" one of my other sisters asked.

And Sister One said, "That? That, my sisters, is music."

I COULD TELL YOU ABOUT what happened next: the stairwell that led us down to a forest of silver, and a forest of diamonds, and a forest of gold. I could tell you about the strange things we saw there, and how we stumbled in a wondrous unison, somehow balletic, all the way through those well-groomed woods until we reached a shore where twelve boats knocked against a dock that stretched out into the water. But all of that is just precursor to what drew us further into that underground world where, in the distance, a castle stood upon an island, illuminated as if by a self-producing glow. Music poured from its high-arched windows like it was the very water that flowed up to the shore to crash upon the sand before us.

It was only then, when the water-music crashed to foam in front of us, that we noticed the young men—our underground princes—waiting in the boats to ferry us across. They were all decked out in tight pants of dark crimson leather and white shirts that opened all the way down to their navels, with gray cloaks thrown over their shoulders like smoke. Their hair, ashen-colored from this distance, curled around their ears. I couldn't help myself. The first thing I did when I saw them was to trace the bare skin at their necks down to their waistlines with my eyes and to swallow hard. The music swarmed around their bodies like sparks, bursting, snapping, and my feet began to twitch involuntarily, my hips to sway like the boats on the water.

Each of us climbed aboard one of the twelve boats and sat at the opposite end from our underground princes, our hands folded in our laps like we were going to still make an attempt at a sense of decorum; and though it probably only took a few minutes to cross that narrow strip of water to the island, I thought I might rend my dress from my body in anticipation of our arrival. I was like a vampire, those creatures of myth I'd read about in the novels I'd read in my father's library. I smelled blood on the air. It was really only the musical notes coming from inside the castle that made me so unnaturally thirsty, but I wanted to lap those notes up like a vampire laps up blood all the same.

Our spooky princes took our hands and walked us away from our boats up the wide stone steps to the front gate of the castle, where the music grew louder and our steps grew lighter, it seemed, the further in we went, as if we had begun to walk on air. We passed through sconce-lit passageways, their fires flickering gold-leaf upon our faces, until suddenly one of the princes stopped at a door that thrummed so hard, it seemed ready to fly off its hinges; and when he opened it, out burst an ear-shattering sound like I had never heard before.

Light—pieces of light—broke into my eyes. On my skin, too, a moment later, light scurried over my flesh as I held my hands out in front of me. When I looked up again, I saw a room full of people, moving to the beat of the music. People of so many different colors wearing so many different strange styles of clothing: silver skirts that hugged their bottoms, earrings that brushed against their collar bones, black lace bras (!), sequined shirts (on men!). They were all dancing, and their movement was as strange as their fashion. They were all either too far apart, throwing their arms into the air or kicking their heels back, or else they were far too close, where no space could be seen between their bodies. Some even pushed their backsides against the waists of their dance partners and, seeing this in particular, I couldn't help but raise my light-speckled hand to my mouth, which hung open like an untended gate.

I laugh at this memory now. I laugh at how innocent I truly was. How little I knew of what the world had to offer beyond the confines of my father's kingdom within its place in time and space. What a gas! What a lark! What a blast! What an epic evening! Even that—all of those bits of language—would have been limited to "Quite enjoyable indeed!" prior to my underground dancehall experiences.

Our spooky princes took our hands and drew us out into the crowded dance floor, where all of us began to move in unfamiliar ways. Our hips out, our hands in the air, our hands gripping those warm bare waistlines of our princes even. The song the DJ was playing kept repeating the phrase, *Get down like you're underground*, and I backed up against my prince, like I'd seen a woman with pink frizzy hair and a face made up like a geisha do with another woman, who was dressed in a dark pinstriped suit and a bowler hat. My prince put his hands on my waist as I ground against him, slid his fingers down my thighs, and for the rest of the night we did not speak a word. We just danced. As one song slid into another, we just sighed.

At the end of that night, my sisters and I knew we'd return. Despite being covered in a slick of our own sweat, despite our dresses and shoes being hopelessly ruined, we knew we'd go back as soon as we could. So after our underground princes led us back to our boats and poled us across the river to the forests of diamonds and of gold and of silver, Sister One stopped at the bottom of the stone steps that led up to our room and said, "Sisters, if we are to ever visit this place again, we must not speak a word of what we saw and what we did this evening. Understand?"

We all nodded, and one by one we made solemn vows. "I will never ever," Sister One said, and then Sister Two, and then Sister Three, and then Sister Four, and so on, down the line we pledged, until it came to me, and I completed the previously unspoken end to our sentence: "I will never ever speak a word of this place or what we do within it."

What happens underground, stays underground.

My sisters all looked at me and grinned. It was one of those moments that, looking back, I can see how I didn't always frustrate them with my innocence, but could sometimes charm them with it.

Which brings a tear to a girl's eye, of course, wading around in the warm pool of good memories. They make one nostalgic though, those comforting waters, and there are plenty of memories that are not so pleasant in all of our histories—so let's move on.

❧

As I recall, our maids and our father were all upset by the state of our dresses and by the ruined remains of our shoes, which we left in a pile in one corner of our room like a heap of garbage. We were questioned over and over, but all of us held fast to our secret. "No, father, I haven't the faintest clue," we all said, feigning ignorance. "We were all asleep and dreaming. Surely someone must be attempting to make a joke of us."

Our father, of course, accepted this excuse. At least he accepted it at first. But as we continued to disappear each night and to return each morning with our new shoes in the same tattered condition as the day before, he grew both wary and weary, and eventually he offered the kingdom one of our hands in marriage to the first man who could uncover the mystery of our shoe-problem.

"Really," said Sister Three on the afternoon of that public announcement, "why does it have to be a man? Why does the reward have to be marriage to one of us? What a jerk. I'm totally getting my drink on tonight. He can't stop me."

"For real," said Sister Nine, and the two of them high-fived each other.

This is when we began drugging those who came to sit in the ante-chamber of our room, so that we could continue going down into the castle beneath our father's castle, where the choice of clubs to visit, we learned soon after returning several times, were infinite.

It was on a night when our spooky princes led us down a different passageway from the one we'd taken on our first few trips that we learned that the underground castle held more rooms to dance in than we'd initially realized, and that each room belonged to a different time and a different space in the world above. Instead of the disco of our first few visits, it was a hip-hop club, and then a country line-dancing bar, and then a death metal hall. Door number one, door number two, door number three, etc. They went on and on down the castle hall, and behind those doors, we could be anyone, we could be anywhere, we could be anywhen.

There was Studio 54, for instance, where our matching sisterly princess dresses made us into immediate stars on the glitter-covered dance floor, and where I discovered the most wonderful substance called angel dust, which I smoked with a beautiful Asian woman whose dyed blond hair surrounded her head like an angel's halo. That evening, I danced with her instead of with my spooky prince, who had slumped down on a couch with his head in the lap of an artist who had become famous in his own time and place for painting soup cans, my prince told me later, as he poled me back across the river. And when we finally reached the stone stairs that would take us up to our room again, my sisters raised their eyebrows at me and tittered playfully about my naughty choice in dance partner. They had already begun to abandon their princes over the course of our nights out, too, much more quickly than I'd dared to do, but they were surprised, I think, to see that I'd done something outside of my usually cautious procedures.

Then there was the Viper Room on Sunset Boulevard (I <3 you Johnny Depp!!), and of course the Copacabana. There was XS in Las Vegas, with that glorious pool in the middle of the floor where we all dove in headfirst and did a tribute to the Busby Berkeley films we'd watched on a dancehall friend's mobile phone one evening over Bloody Mary's at an all-night diner. We touched the bottom of that pool and watched the bubbles of air escape our mouths to rise to the top of the water, which we burst through a moment later, crossing our hands above us, over and over, to the roaring applause of our fellow clubbers.

And there was the Roxy. And—oh my God—the Ministry of Sound in London. Whiskey A Go-Go, where I drank far too much whiskey and go-goed myself into a silly stupor, was sick all the next day and stayed in bed, nursed by Sister Eight, who had decided not to drink that night and made sure to bring us apple juice for breakfast and chicken broth for lunch and told our father we'd all caught the same illness after drinking water from a brook in a nearby forest.

Womb, in Tokyo. Wow, that night's a broken mirror. CBGB's, when we were feeling punk and wanted to tease our hair up into Frankenstein's wife's crazy beehives and wear jeans with holes in our knees. Berghain in Berlin—oh Lord, you don't even want to know the shit I saw go down in some of the rooms of that former power plant gone fetish leather. They only played techno in there, and the place was nothing but dark room after dark room with strobe lights blinding you momentarily. Luckily Sister Six scored us some ecstasy and all was good after we swallowed those smiley-faced pills.

There was the Paradise Garage, too, of course, which my sisters were fond of because it was located on King Street. They thought it was clever to go dancing at a club that reminded us of our father, who was totally tearing his hair out about our ruined shoes and constant daytime sleeping at that point, not to mention all of the would-be suitors he kept having to behead when they couldn't discover the mystery of our ruined shoes each morning. We felt bad about our suitors' deaths, my sisters and I, but honestly, they should have minded their own business and left my father to do his own dirty work. And really, what kind of idiot tries to follow in the footsteps of the multiple men who had tried before him and ended up beheaded? Clearly, they weren't the brightest of the bulbs in the kingdom.

It was the Limelight, though—this old church turned club in the heart of Manhattan—that stole my heart more than any other club we went to. There, my sisters and I came with our faces painted to look like butterfly wings, or like strange monsters. We wore purple or blue long, stringy wigs, and ripped up our princess dresses so that we looked like down-and-out rich girls who got lost on their way home from the prom and were led astray by big bad wolves instead of knights in shining armor. The music was techno and industrial, the drugs were always upbeat. The mirror ball in the center of the dance floor spun and broke light against our painted faces, like that first night we'd gone dancing in the underground castle, and oh, everyone there was so ready to laugh and twirl and pretend to be somebody that they weren't in real life.

I understood that, the pretending. Back home in my father's kingdom, we were quiet and reserved. We bowed and we handed over our hands to men who kissed them, and we batted away compliments as if we were not worthy of praise. We ate only a third of what was put on our plates for dinner, and we drank only one glass of wine in front of anyone. At social occasions, we danced with old men who would slip their hands around our waists like we belonged to them; and when we pulled away, they would raise their brows and question us about whether or not we wanted to upset our father.

Politics. Fuck politics. My sisters and I had found our own kingdom to belong to. And at the Limelight, that Gothic-styled church in the middle of Manhattan, we could feel like we were still in our father's kingdom but also in our new home, among the party monsters with whom we shared our revels.

❦

THE SAD THING IS, OUR story is a fairy tale. That can't be dismissed. And no matter what anyone tells you about fairy tales, most of them don't really have happy endings. Not the real fairy tales, that is. Not the ones that really happened.

What happened to us was, the old soldier I've already mentioned came to my father's castle and took up the challenge to find out how our shoes would come to be ruined every night like a ritual, and he had a couple of things going for him that the beheaded suitors before him hadn't. He had that cloak of invisibility the old crone in the woods gave him, for instance, and the advice she'd also given when he told her he was going to take up the king's challenge: *Don't drink the cup of wine they'll give you at the end of the night, but make them think that you did.*

Old crone, wherever you are, I will totally slap you across the face for this treachery if ever I come across you. What did we ever do to you? Did you hate us because we were happy?

So the soldier found us out. Didn't drink the drugged wine we gave him. Pretended to fall asleep. Put the cloak of invisibility over his shoulders and followed us down into the forests of silver and gold and diamonds. Slipped onto the boat with my spooky prince and me. Saw us dancing with an array of unseemly characters at the Limelight. Saw me with too much vodka and a little bit of pot in my system, lifting up my dress in the middle of the dance floor. Jesus, that was a great night, regardless of what followed.

The thing was, I knew someone was shadowing us that night, I just couldn't see him. I knew it and twice I said to my sisters, "Something is wrong here. I feel as though someone unseen is among us."

And of course my sisters either pursed their lips skeptically or threw their heads back in laughter. "Stop worrying!" they said. "You're such a downer!"

But he found us out, that soldier, and he explained our secret to our father the very next morning, after we returned, before we could even put ourselves to bed and pretend like we didn't know what he was talking about.

"My daughters," our father said when he learned of what we'd been doing. "How dare you sneak about like thieves in the night? How dare you dance with anyone who offers a hand like a common harlot?"

"But father—" Sister Ten said, clasping her hands together as if she were praying.

"Enough!" our father thundered, and we all cringed, wishing our mother had not died in my childbirth, for it would have been nice to have a mother there right then to soften our father in this moment. "Your underground nights have ended," he told us. "And you will no longer live in this room. It will be sealed off, in fact, and starting tomorrow, one of you will marry each month until a year has passed and all of you are living a proper life. I've been too easy on you all. Let you now answer to husbands!"

He let the old soldier pick which of us he wanted to marry, like we were the carcasses of dead chickens hanging up in a shopkeeper's window. Which one is the plumpest, the juiciest? My oldest sister, of course, Sister One, who he'd been eyeing up the entire time my father scolded us.

Father married her off to the old soldier the next day. The eleven of us were her bridesmaids. Most of us looked down at our feet as Sister One made her vows to the old soldier. We put the tips of our fingers to our eyes to wipe away any tears before they might show.

AFTER THAT, I WATCHED EACH of my other sisters married off to dukes and lords and even one was given to a blacksmith whose work my father admired. We were his property, traded and bartered with for political gain and finely crafted weapons. It was as if he were preparing to go to war with an enemy that had not yet revealed its existence. I suppose we were his enemies. Our betrayal of his trust made us disgusting to him.

Each wedding was a brief and sad affair, except for when it came to Sister Eleven's. By then nearly a year had passed and she had had time to get used to the idea of this inevitability, and had persuaded my father to at least allow her some consideration in the selection of her husband. My father appreciated Sister Eleven's embrace of her fate, and allowed her to choose between three suitors of his picking. I suppose that was an option of sorts. Sister Eleven knew to accept this and not to dare complain.

They married in the spring, under a blossoming cherry tree.

I was next, of course, but unlike Sister Eleven, I had not become accustomed to the idea of marriage as punishment, even if I could choose between a handful of my father's selections. All those months barred from the underground castle, I tossed and turned on my bed, thinking of the many people with whom I had danced and the many experiences I had enjoyed (even the bad ones), and burned as if I had a fever. And on the night of Sister Eleven's wedding, when I cried out in my sleep while I dreamed someone was suffocating me with a pillow, I knew I could not do as my father commanded. I knew I would once again have to betray him.

MY FATHER HAD HAD THE door to our old bedroom barred shut from the outside, and a guard patrolled that hall now more often than they used to. So it would be no use trying to pry the door open. I only had one real option. I would have to climb up the vines that covered the wall on that side of the castle, and flit through our old room's window like a moth.

I waited until the eve of my wedding, which was to be a marriage with a middle-aged archduke who smelled of horse dung and had brown spots on his teeth, and when the clouds passed over the moon of that early summer night, casting everything in darkness for several minutes, I began my ascent.

Hand over hand, foot braced in the nooks and crannies of the thick vines on the wall, I made my way up to the windowsill within fifteen minutes, just before my arms grew so sore I thought I might fall, and had only enough energy to pull myself over the ledge and drop down into our old bedroom, where the thud of my landing echoed through the lifeless room.

Before me were our empty beds, the covers pulled up and made as if they were waiting for someone to return to them, as if the girls that usually inhabited them were just out for the night, dancing, and any minute now they would come running up the stairs from the underground forest of silver, holding their laughter tighter as they ascended, and would finally put themselves to bed. I nearly cried, remembering how it had been not so long ago, recalling the feeling of freedom.

But I didn't let myself waste too much time, and quickly went to the stone door and placed my palm upon it, sighed with relief as it began to grind and lower itself to reveal the stone staircase that would lead me back to the underground castle. Back to my spooky prince, who minutes later caught me in his arms as I ran toward him, out of breath, then poled me across the river, where we ran up the stairs of the underground castle, our hands linked between us, and disappeared into the dark of the cavernous entrance.

IN A CASTLE UNDERGROUND, IN a place where time and space don't exist in the ways that we're used to, a person doesn't age. You just are. You exist, but outside of the laws of nature. I spent the timeless passage of what would have been years for someone locked into a particular world doing nothing but dancing. I went to all of my sisters' and my favorite clubs, night after endless night, and slept my days away in a room not unlike our old bedroom. A hostel sort of room, it was, where the homeless types like me who had taken up residence in the underground castle would go to sleep when they didn't go home with a dance partner from another world for the evening. We were fugitives from our own circumstances, fleeing the cage of fate in which our origins would entrap us.

My sisters all got married. That's the end of their stories, like all the bad punch lines to all the bad knock-knock jokes that somehow still manage to breathe in the world. A typical fairy tale ending, only not so happily after all.

But me? My ending is different. I picked the lock on time and space, and escaped my fate to live outside of the rules of a particular world. I live alone, but at least I'm free.

I've seen so many worlds now. I've seen so many things since I became a wanderer. And though I often feel the weight of guilt lower upon my shoulders when I think of my poor sisters back in my father's realm, married off to husbands who are little more than jailors, I can't say I'd do anything different. I feel the guilt, and then I accept it. I confess this great sin—the fact that there's no way I could have lived out the ending of their fairy tales, that I abandoned them to the fate I would have been assigned as well—and roll it all up as a message in a bottle.

The river that flows by the underground castle flows through all the worlds in all the times that exist in the universe. I cast the bottle into it and watch my story bob as it floats its way into eternity. And then I turn, called by the music in the castle to return to it.

One day, if you find these words and read them, know that I have quite a different ending than my sisters. Know that I'm happy, despite having to call myself a person who has run away.

And if you ever find your own secret passage into the underground, you can be sure that I'll be the girl you see in every club you ever visit. The one on the floor with the mirror ball spinning above her, showering light down on her hair and shoulders as she twirls and whirls. I'll be the one who never stops dancing.

Men usually
grow base by
degrees. From me,
in an instant, all virtue
dropped bodily as a mantle.
From comparatively trivial
wickedness I passed, with the stride
of a giant, into more than the enormities of
an Elah-Gabalus. What chance—what one
event brought this evil thing to pass, bear
with me while I relate. Death approaches;
and the shadow which foreruns him has thrown
a softening influence over my spirit. I long, in passing
through the dim valley, for the sympathy—I had nearly
said for the pity—of my fellow men. I would fain have
them believe that I have been, in some measure, the slave of
circumstances beyond human control. I would wish them to
seek out for me, in the details I am about to give, some little
oasis of fatality amid a wilderness of error. I would have them
allow—what they cannot refrain from allowing—that,
although temptation may have erewhile existed
as great, man was never thus, at least, tempted
before—certainly, never thus fell. And is it
therefore that he has never thus suffered? Have I not
indeed been living in a dream? And am I not now dying
a victim to the horror and the mystery of the wildest of all
sublunary visions?

WILLIAM WILSON.
EDGAR ALLAN POE.
1839

FOR THE APPLAUSE OF SHADOWS

IT IS TRUE THAT MY voice could not be raised above the sound of a whisper, and that I was not the sort of person who received attention or applause for anything I might say or do, but that is where my Other's ability to tell the truth began and ended. I would call him the prince of lies, if only that title did not seem so crowned with a certain glory and purpose. And purpose was one thing my Other's deceitful behavior lacked. He could only have enjoyed ruining the lives of innocent people. He could only have taken pleasure from the believed lies he told. From where I stand now, though, speculating on his reasoning does not matter. In the world below, I pass my endless hours climbing the shaft of a cavern that leads up to the blue-aired realm; and when one finds oneself thrown into Death's oubliette, cast off from the world, the motivations of the Other William Wilson are neither here nor there.

Or, if his motivations do matter, it is only when I chance to see his face in the swirling mists that fill the cavern entrance, where I am able to stand and observe the world's continuous spinning. Not a foot beyond the cave mouth, where the stones crop up like sharp teeth, am I permitted. But what I see from here is quite more than one might at first assume. Like a reflecting pool, images fill the cavern entrance, and the occurrences of the world are delivered like strange yet familiar dreams. And they are such exquisitely painful dreams, the dreams of the living. They make me ache and stretch out my hands, unwittingly grasping after what has been taken from me.

There is no fiercer punishment than being shown what you desire but cannot possess.

❦

"WE'RE ALIKE, YOU AND I."

Those were the first words I can recall him saying to me. Clearly they could not be the very first words he had ever said to me, though, because how would he have known we were alike if we had never spoken? But my memory of the other William Wilson before this particular statement is vague. What I remember is that we were in the same school, that our principal was the reverend Dr. Bransby, who ruled with a Draconian bent in the classrooms yet spoke the language of angels during his Sunday sermons. And I remember how William Wilson was one of the more intelligent among my classmates. He had always attracted attention, had always been lauded by our teachers and our classmates for his quick and cutting tongue, had always received more accolades and applause than I, who could barely raise my voice above the level of a whisper, had ever known.

He had dark eyes with dark circles beneath them, hair that curled around his temples like a crown of black ivy, the lips of a cherub, carved and smooth as stone.

When he leaned across the space between our desks that day to whisper, "We're alike, you and I," and I felt his lips brush against the curve of my ear, it was as if he'd blown life into me, and I awoke, right then, right there, into a room full of young men paying attention to their lesson, as if I was the other William Wilson's own creation, an eidolon he had dreamed into being, and when I turned to face him, I found him staring at me with the most delicious grin.

"How?" I said, even softer than normal, and my word drifted across the space between us like the seed of a dandelion.

Before he could answer, though, our teacher slammed a book upon his lectern. "Mr. Wilson," he shouted, "what is it that you think you are doing?"

We both turned to face him, not knowing which of us he meant, or if he meant both. In the end, though, it was my Other who spoke.

"Nothing, sir," he said, shaking his head innocently, that delicious grin wiped clean off his face. "I was just encouraging Wilson here to speak up when he answers your questions. He's quite brilliant, sir, don't you think?"

Our teacher neither smiled nor dignified the question with an answer. His white brows furrowed, and his forehead wrinkled like a washboard. I could see his lips held tight together, trembling to unleash a tumult of outrage, yet he did not lash out at my Other as he might have done so easily. Instead, he told us to resume our attention, and then he returned to speaking in the monotone voice for which he was known and about which the students joked after returning to our sleeping quarters in the evenings.

I sat quiet and attentive in my seat, still anxious that I would be associated with trouble due to my Other's instigations, but as our teacher returned to his lecture, I turned to find my Other staring at me once more with that delicious smile curling to reveal his teeth.

"Tonight," he mouthed silently, and though he did not make a sound, I heard the word in my ear as if his lips were still there, still brushing against me.

❧

I SPENT THE REST OF that day in the long narrow room in which all of our studies were conducted, where high Gothic arched windows

FOR THE APPLAUSE OF SHADOWS

reached to the ceiling, and light filtered down through the panes of glass, illuminating the dust in the air. I did not break and take fresh air with the others that afternoon, but continued to sit at my desk, riddled as it was with the carved names of long forgotten students and the vague images of grotesqueries that I could never comprehend, no matter how long I stared at their overlapping lines and strangely bulbous proportions. I worked at a mathematics problem we'd been given earlier.

Ordinarily I would go outside, where the youngest of the students, the ten-year-olds, chased after one another as if they were still children, and where the oldest, the fifteen-year-olds, coolly went off in packs, or walked round the grounds two-by-two with a favorite friend. That day, though, I could not join the others. Not after what my Other had said aloud about my inability to speak above the sound of a whisper. It was the one thing, the very one thing, that I had no control over, and about which I wanted no attention. Yet he had brought attention to it, making me hate him a little, even as I trembled at the touch of his breath on my skin. That feeling of being stirred into being, that feeling of having been awakened into the dream of life for the first time, made me look at him as if it were the first I had ever seen him.

It was a strange feeling for many reasons, but especially because my Other and I *had* known each other for several years already, since we first entered Dr. Bransby's school on the very same day and were found to be interesting by all because we shared the same birthday and because we shared the same name. Our features, too, were remarkably similar, and sometimes, because of our shared name, scholars in the upper forms wondered if we were related. We both took any opportunity to assure them that we held no connexions beyond the queer coincidence of our names and birthdates and our similarly timed entrances to Dr. Bransby's school, but it was the other William Wilson who took particular delight in clarifying any misconception about our relationship whenever the occasion arose. "*Him?*" I once heard him say in response to an older student. "Never. No. We may share a name, and that name is unfortunately, pathetically common, I admit, but I am not common like *that one*."

He spoke so loudly during this exchange that I knew he meant to shame me publicly, to sever any potential associations others might perceive.

So when he leaned across the space between us that morning to tell me we were alike, I could not comprehend his motives. Was it another cruel joke at my expense? Was it a way for him to bring our teacher's attention to us only so he could mention my weak voice while he had the attention of every boy in our form?

By the time I heard footsteps creaking across the floorboards behind my desk, I had worked myself into such a state of paranoia that when I felt a hand land upon my shoulder, I jumped from my seat and nearly spun in place, my fear had grown so outsized, the way a shadow thrown against a wall is sometimes larger than its owner.

It was only our teacher, though, returning. "Mr. Wilson," he said. "Why do you not join the others?"

I blinked, not knowing what to say, as I could not tell him the truth of the matter. Eventually, though, I found my inner resources and replied. "I was studying my mathematics." I then looked down at the desk where my work was displayed.

"You must give your mind time to rest," my teacher said. "Otherwise you will exhaust it. Go outside now. Join the others."

He nodded toward the high arched windows, and I turned to see a scene of boys mingling out in the chill of an autumn day, leaves swirling like bright stars between them. I gathered my coat and left the halls of the mansion for the cold air of the school grounds, where I did not join the others but instead walked the perimeter of the stone walls that surrounded the school, pausing when I reached the wrought-iron front gates that sealed us in, as though we were prisoners, to peer through the black bars at the outside world.

How like life my death is. Walled in by stone. But here in my cavern below the world, I am not as confined as I had been by Dr. Bransby's walls and wrought iron. I cannot only see the aboveworld from my cavern entrance, I can also reach out into the occurrences swirling before me, and sometimes I can grasp hold of the life that's been denied me, the way one can reach into the recesses of the mind, fumbling in the depths of dark water, only to find the form of a submerged memory and pull it ashore like the body of a drowned person.

❦

I WAS NOT MADE TO wait much longer to understand what my Other truly wanted. He had mouthed the word *tonight*, and indeed that night he appeared to me as a white face suddenly hovering over my own as I lay in bed, surfacing from sleep, and I opened my mouth to gasp for breath that would not come due to the shock of his sudden appearance.

"Shhh," he said, placing one rough-skinned finger against my lips. "You mustn't make a sound, William."

It was possibly the first time he had ever called me by our given name without referencing our surname. It was, at least, the first time I ever took notice. Perhaps it was the way the moonlight fell through the window beside my bed and lay across his features like a sheer veil, illuminating his pale skin, darkening his dark eyes and dark hair, that made me want to comply with his order, because I did as instructed and did not make a sound beyond the gentle intake of breath that flew from my body as he pulled back my covers and slipped in beside me, pulling them up again, pulling them over us, so that we were encased in them, floating in the dark beneath them, where no moonlight could reach us.

In that darkness, his hands roamed across the bridge of my nose, the crevasse of my lips, the hollow of my neck, where he eventually lowered his mouth to kiss me. Then across my chest and down to my stomach, where his hands lingered, his fingertips softly drawing circles through the downy hair that grew there.

"It's much better like this." His voice was soft as he lowered his hand further, caressing me.

"How?" I whispered, as I had that morning.

"In the dark," he said, "when I cannot see you, it is like you are myself, only you are another. Another me. You are my other."

Then his fingers slipped even further and I was gasping again.

Gasping even as he stroked me and held me close with his other arm and pulled at the skin of my neck with his teeth.

THE NEXT DAY I FOUND him in the dining hall eating breakfast, just as I would have on any other morning, but as I sat across the long table from him and met his eyes, he did not reveal any subtle indication, did not share an intimate look that only I would comprehend, to acknowledge what had passed between us. Instead, he looked at me as if it had been a long night of perpetual rain, and the worms had been washed out of the earth and onto the flagstones, wriggling beneath his dreadful notice.

"What are you looking at?" he muttered. His voice was acid thrown upon me, and I withered, my mouth gaping open without reply. "Oh, Wilson," he said, cringing at the mention of our shared name. "Do not be so petulant. It does not become *you* of all people."

Other scholars were scraping back chairs now, joining us at the table, and I closed my mouth but could not refrain from frowning. *How?* I wanted to ask. *How can you treat me in this cold manner, after everything you said? After everything you did to me?*

He did not give me attention throughout that dismal meal, nor later, when we sat through our lectures. He did not lean across the space between us to whisper into my ear no matter how I wished him to do so. I thought I might force my will into his body, like a hand into a glove, and puppet him through the motions I wanted, which were only a repetition of what he had already said and done the night before.

But it was my Other who was the puppeteer, and I his stringed instrument, jangling at the twitch of his fingers.

He would come to me again despite the coldness he directed at me, like a blast of winter wind, in the days that followed his nighttime visitations. Again and again, he would appear at the foot of my bed during the midnight hour, staring down at my pale body in the moonlight, which I would display for him each time he came, as if I were placing myself on an altar.

Take me. Let me feel our lips together, our hands entwined, let me feel you press against my thigh.

I trembled at his touch, unable to muster any of the anger he evoked in the days that came after our secret meetings, when he would look right through me, as if I were merely the ghost of his own shadow thrown against the wall.

I hated him. I loved him. I wanted to pinch out the flame of his life between my thumb and forefinger.

But it was he who accomplished the snuffing out, it was he who anticipated my wild emotions, which had, over the months of our secret nights together, admittedly grown into raucous and rapidly shifting forms. Now I was calm, now I was furious. Now I was sober, now obsessively curious. I began to do things even I had not anticipated in my character, as if there were another me hiding within my body, aching to enter the world, to do the work I could not bring myself to do in daylight.

He caught me in his room one day in late autumn. I was going through the drawers of his dressing table, examining the remnants of his existence as though they might provide me with a substitute for him during the periods when he would absent himself from my bed. "What are you doing in here, Wilson?" he said, his voice as firm as Dr. Bransby's whenever he punished a student who had provided him with a case for severe disappointment. His silhouette crowded the doorway.

I pushed shut the drawer I'd been searching through before I turned to face him, and for a moment I could say nothing, could only feel the heat of my shame rise up through my body and burn me. And then, quite unexpectedly, even to myself, I said a dangerous thing.

"I love you."

My Other, though, simply sneered at this admission. Then, shaking his head, he crossed the room and slapped me once, hard, across my face. "Wake up," he said, as if he himself had not been the one to awaken me in the night, as if he were not the one who had awakened me into these feelings. "Get out of my room. Get out this instant."

I crept like an insect to his doorway, but looked back over my shoulder to utter yet another dangerous thing before leaving.

"I will tell," I whispered to the other William Wilson. "I will tell all of them what you have done. I will tell everyone what we have done together."

I remained for no more than a moment to enjoy the fear that passed across his face like wind rippling the still waters of a lake, and then I fled as though I were going to carry out my threat that very minute.

It took my Other mere seconds to catch up to me in the hallway. Breathlessly, he turned me around to face him. His hands gripping my forearms, he said, "Do not tell, William. There is no need to destroy what is between us. I am sorry for my ill treatment. Would you forgive me? Please? I beg you."

These words, they sang in my ears and lifted my heart and cleansed me of any poisonous feelings.

"Yes," I said, and nearly put my arms around him there, where anyone might have seen us. "All is forgiven," I told him.

"Good." He smiled, his dark eyes lit with a gleam. "I will come to you tonight then," he said, and I nodded. He was going to give himself to me, as I had given myself to him, over and over.

❧

I WAITED IN MY ROOM for him to come that night, anticipating the meeting of our conjoined souls, and when eventually, hours later, my door creaked open, I sat up in bed and parted the curtains for him to enter.

No moon hung in my window that night, but my Other carried a lamp with him. Normally he would leave the lamp with a shade upon it outside, as he had always enjoyed the loss of self that darkness provided. Now, though, he crossed my floor with lamp in hand to stand above me, the curtain pulled aside, and gazed down upon my body with eyes that might devour me. When finally he placed a shade over the lamp and darkness fell like a mantle throughout the room, I held my breath, waiting to feel his body slip in beside me; and when he did join me, and I felt his hand on my hip, I sighed.

My Other began to stroke first my shoulder, then my cheek with just one finger, then my throat. I yearned for the burn of his feverish hands to mark me, but before I realized what, exactly, he wanted that night, it was too late. His touch in the dark had deceived me, as his words deceived any he encountered, and what had been just a single finger against my shoulder, what had been just the back of his hand rolling across my cheek, suddenly became a vice around my throat as he pressed me down with one hand and found a pillow with the other, which he placed over me, pressing down hard, then harder.

Even if I might have screamed, no one would have heard me. My voice—my voice that could not rise above the sound of a whisper—would have never reached them in that labyrinthine mansion.

WITH MY FINAL BREATH SQUEEZED from me, I awoke in the land of shades, and stumbled my way through the caverns that led down to the heart of the underworld, where, when I reached its center, I found my lady greeting her newest subjects from a throne of broken bones. Her face was white as a powdered wig, her lips red as blood, her hair, black and writhing like the snakes of Medusa. There were so many shades gathered around her, so many lost souls wandering her hollowed-out kingdom, but when I approached to kneel, she raised her hand and said, "You are not a shadow, young one. Will still clings to your mind. Tell me, how did you come to me in this way, with so much life left in you?"

I told her my story, which I could see she could not help but enjoy from the wicked grin that lifted her cheeks at the various turnings in its telling. And as her pleasure became apparent to her subjects, they began to take an interest as well: murmuring their dissent when I told them of the other William Wilson's deception, raising their voices into a frenzy of outrage as I closed the story with the other William Wilson's hand closing upon my neck as he pressed a pillow to me.

When finally I fell silent, Lady Death lifted her strong chin and said, "You, my young one, have been wronged," and her shadow minions threw their fists above their heads, demanding justice. But when Lady

Death scanned the room, they fell silent again. She turned to me then, her hair coiling about her face, and said, "If you could set your death right, would you?"

Without hesitation I spoke. "Yes," I told her. And for the first time ever, my voice was not a whisper, but loud as it tolled and echoed through my lady's caverns, growing louder and broader as it swept away from me.

Then the shades and lost souls threw their fists into the air again and cheered.

Lady Death looks kindly upon the world's victims. "Here," she said, and tied a black silken mask to my face as a wife might arrange a corsage in her husband's buttonhole. "You are bound to this place, but so long as you wear this, you may pass among the living as one of them on occasion. Go now. Claim your vengeance. For yourself and for your new queen."

Up the shaft of the cavern I went after receiving the mask. Up that steep incline I traveled until I reached the cavern entrance where I had been born into darkness. And there, for the first time since my exit from the world, in the mists that filled the entrance, I saw my Other continuing to live and breathe, his existence as serene as still water.

He had left school not long after my death and returned to his family—shocked, his father explained to the reverend Dr. Bransby, by the loss of his friend who had died so suddenly and mysteriously in his sleep—and would eventually be sent on to school in Eton, where he could start over properly.

If only everyone were given such new beginnings, the world would be a fairer place. As it stands, though, only the ruthless, like my Other, enjoy such grace, and only because they take what they want by any means: through deception, theft, and rape.

❦

THROUGH THE MISTS OF THE cavern entrance I watched him, waiting for my memory to grow cold and stiff in the recesses of his mind, biding my endless time while he continued to drink himself into stupors, gamble away his fortune, steal from his classmates at Eton who did not yet suspect the evil among them—until I felt my lips rise on either side, and was quite certain that I had come upon the perfect moment in which I could begin my vindication.

On a night when William Wilson and his friends were carousing, drinking and throwing cards upon the table of his room, I fixed Lady Death's mask upon my face and stepped through the mists of my cavern entrance, only to find myself in the outer hall of my Other's chambers, where his servant asked for my name. "I am an old friend," I told the servant. "If you would permit me, I would like to surprise him."

The servant had grown used to my Other's strange and profligate behavior, so my wish was not so out of the ordinary, and he opened the chamber door and announced the presence of a guest waiting for his master in the outer vestibule.

From within the chamber, the sounds of raucous laughter rolled out into the hallway. "Who could it be? Who could it be, knocking upon my door so late in the evening?" I heard my Other ask his guests in a theatrical manner. But as he crossed the threshold of his rooms and saw me standing in the vestibule, wearing the same clothing he himself wore, thanks to the illusion my mask conjured, his face twisted in a most delightfully frightening manner, and he stood frozen.

Before he could turn back and close his door upon me, I left the vestibule and rushed to him. Placing my hands upon his forearms, the way he had held my own that day several years ago, when he had lied in the form of an apology and begged for forgiveness, I leaned in closer to him, thrust my finger toward his eyes, and hissed the words he most dreaded.

"William Wilson."

So frightened by my apparition was my Other than he nearly fainted in my arms. He stumbled against the wall in a weak attempt to escape, and by the time he gathered his disordered wits, I had retreated to the vestibule and returned through the morning mist to my cavern.

Gone. I had disappeared into the mist as if *I* were the mist, as if I had been a figure of his imagination sprung to life for no more than an instant.

HE RAN FROM THAT MOMENT, as he had run from Dr. Bransby's school after taking my life. He believed he could outrun the truth of his existence—that he was a liar who took pleasure in ruining the lives of others—and so he went on to Oxford, where his family provided him with an establishment so great he was able to appear as the noblest of commoners among those whose hereditary fortunes made them into giants.

When I next intruded on him, he was cheating a young nobleman out of his family fortune in a game of spades. The nobleman was a good sort. I could tell by the way he and his friends got along in decent fashion, liberally making gentle jests at each other's expense, and I could tell by the way he grew flushed by his liquor much earlier than any other in the room, and how his words began to slur sooner than the others as well. His hair was the color of sand, but it draped around his face like silk, and his skin was as delicate and white as a porcelain doll. I wanted to lean out of the cavern entrance, to brush a finger against that ivory cheek, and almost succeeded in convincing myself that I might use my mask's illusions to carry out other unfulfilled desires, but I was stopped from indulging when I heard my Other offer to pour more wine for the table. Never before had I heard him offer to do something for others unless it was somehow to his own advantage.

By then, late into the night, the party members were already leaning one way or another in their chairs, or were holding themselves up by placing an arm across the fireplace mantel. My Other, though, appeared in good health as he stood from his chair and made his way to the next bottle, which he opened with a flourish while making a jest over his shoulder at someone else's inability to drink any longer. As he turned back to pouring the wine into their glasses, though, I saw him slip a small vile from his sleeve, which he uncapped and, from it, poured a powder into my porcelain nobleman's glass. This, I realized, was how he had gotten the young man so much more confused by his wine than any other person that evening. And it was but one of his strategies for cheating the boy out of his fortune.

I, too, was drunk that evening. Watching the young nobleman, I sipped at his beauty and felt a flicker of life course through my dead flesh for the first time since I had come to the land of shades. I wanted him. Not the other William Wilson but the young nobleman, who seemed kind and good, and whose features reminded me of seraphim. I wanted to wrap my arms around his back and press my face against in his smooth chest, a portion of which appeared after he had grown hot and unbuttoned the top three holes. So when I noticed my Other subtly preparing to destroy him, I stepped out of the cavern as if it were my own life I were protecting, and burst through the doors of my nobleman's chambers, extinguishing the candles in the room with the force of my entrance. And within that dimly lit, smoke-filled room, I exposed my Other.

"Please to examine," I told those startled young men, "at your leisure, the inner linings of the cuff of this man's left sleeve, and the several little packages which may be found in the somewhat capacious pockets of his embroidered morning wrapper."

Immediately the young men took him into their many hands and divested him of his deceitful instruments—the black court cards he had placed up his sleeves that allowed him to keep winning—and my young nobleman who had nearly lost his fortune proved the greatness of his nobility by warning my Other to quit Oxford on the morrow, no more and no less.

And so the other William Wilson, cloak in hand, freed from punishment by the nobility of others, ran once again.

I remained after he had exited, lingering behind my young nobleman's figure by the window as he watched my Other flee across the lawn. I wanted to lean into him, to put my hands upon his large shoulders, to place a kiss upon his neck, to see him turn to me and feel the fall of his warm breath on my face before he pulled me to him. But it was impossible. With my Other gone, I was no more than a shadow. My young nobleman could no longer see me. Lady Death's mask was a gift for only one purpose.

So I left my young nobleman and my desires behind, and returned to the mists, where I began to look once again for the fleeing William Wilson. Wherever he ran to, I would find him. From the mists of the cavern entrance, I would go forth and come to haunt his days. In Paris, in Berlin, in Rome, in Vienna. In Moscow and Naples, even in Egypt. Wherever he went, there I was, his shadow, brushing my lips against the curve of his ear, whispering his own name, the name he hated with the dread one reserves for the sight of a spectre.

❦

"Why is it that you wait, young one?"

The question came as a surprise, as I had been incessantly watching the mist, and my Other within it, grinding out his days. I turned to find Lady Death standing in the shadows, where the cavern began its decline into the underworld. No smile lit her gray face though. No fire surged in the black furnaces of her eyes. When I looked down at my own feet without an answer for her, she came forward, put the tip of her finger beneath my chin, and lifted my face.

"We think we know why you wait," my lady said softly.

I had no reply, though this time I was forced to look into the cold and cobwebbed sockets of her eyes.

"It is because of our gift to you," she said, touching the silken black mask that had grown to be such a part of my own face that I had nearly forgotten it. "You've fallen in love with the illusions it provides. Though remember, young one, the illusions are meant to aid you in the taking of your vengeance, not to comfort you with a fantasy that you yet live. Death is where you dwell now, and Death is where you will remain, however much the mask allows you to partake in life again, if only for brief moments. You cannot remain in this in-between place forever, parting these mists for your own pleasure. You owe us fealty. Carry out your desire, or we shall be forced to retract our gift and that, unfortunately, would be most unsatisfying for both of us, as we and our shadows do so love retribution."

"I am sorry, my lady," I said, nodding, and she removed the tip of her finger from my chin.

"Good," she said, and then she began to walk backward, slowly at first, then quicker and quicker, as if it were the most natural direction, and I stood there watching, as any loyal subject should, until her face melted into darkness and she was gone.

❦

IT WAS IN ROME, DURING the Carnival of 18—, at a masquerade thrown in the palazza of an old and enfeebled Neopolitan duke, where I next found my Other lifting more glasses from the wine table than any other guest. The affair was a large one, made even larger by the grandiosity of the guests' costumes and masks, some of which seemed like the wings of a black butterflies, flitting about the room, alighting here on one person's and then another's shoulder. Laughter shot up through the room like fountains, and music from the duke's ensemble wove between the loud and raucous voices like water through rock.

Taking a last swallow of wine from his glass, my Other began to weave his way among the crowd, though it was clear by the sweat on his brow and the strain on his face that he had little patience in him. And with good reason, as it was his mistress to whom he was making his way; and after having so freely imbibed so much of the wine table's contents, he wanted to reach her as soon as possible, to quench the fire he'd built within himself so early in the evening.

His mistress was the wife of the old duke, a younger bride who was kind to the old doter, but who arranged for other, more passionate relationships at her leisure. She had informed the other William Wilson about her costume choices a day prior, in a note sent in secrecy, or what she had thought was secrecy, so that he could find her and take her to a small ante-chamber adjoining the ball-room to have their way. This was the time. I knew as soon as I saw the note pass from her servant's hand to my Other's. This was the time for my final revenge upon my murderer.

He had just glimpsed her between the heads and shoulders of the crowded room, and was about to cross the floor to meet her, when I placed my gloved hand upon his shoulder and leaned down to whisper in his ear.

"William Wilson," I whispered, and immediately he spun around to seize me roughly by my collar.

"Scoundrel!" he said through gritted teeth. "Who are you? How do you come to haunt me? How do you come to *seem* like me, to wear my very own costume?"

Before I could answer, though, he pushed me through a door of one of the surrounding ante-chambers, where he had intended to consummate the affair with his mistress, and thrust the door shut behind him.

"You *shall not* dog me forever, imposter!" he shouted, and drew his sword.

"I am no imposter." I drew my own sword, laying my edge against his.

The wine he had so freely taken slowed him, and so his wits were not only dull but also frantic from the heat of his temper. He came at me again and again, thrusting his sword wildly, attempting to push me against the wainscoting; but, tripping over his own feet, he fell to the floor, where I finally plunged my sword into his bosom once, twice, thrice, until his clothes were stained with blossoms of blood as it left him.

As his will, defeated, began to leave him, I knelt next to him, and heard him murmuring these words: "You have conquered, and I yield. Yet, henceforward art thou also dead—dead to the World, to Heaven and Hope! In me didst thou exist—and, in my death, see by this image, which is thine own, how utterly thou hast murdered thyself."

Ravings. Ravings of a mind that had always been turned inward. Never once had he seen me standing before him, now or in the past, not even in my own bed during his midnight visitations. Only a reflection of himself could he behold, wherever he cast his eyes. Even now, as he began to rehearse his dying breath, his perceptions twisted and curled through the room like a thorny vine.

I could not abide it, for what vengeance would I accomplish if he could not see his own murderer truly.

So I lowered my lips to his ear for one last time.

"Self-deceiver," I said. "That sword you believe you have placed into your own gut, that blood that comes flowing from the cut: that is not your hand, nor your own self-imposed justice for your wrong-doings. It is my own sweet vengeance, and the hand that twists the blade, that hand upon the hilt, is my own and no other's."

From behind me, I heard first the slow and solemn clapping of Lady Death's hands coming together from where she sat upon her throne of broken bones below, watching, as she is always watching—me, you, everyone—and then the mask she had gifted me dropped away like an autumn leaf, its life expended.

I turned then, stood, and raised my hands above me, awash in the applause that the shadows rained upon me.

She cried, "Laura," up the garden,
"Did you miss me?
Come and kiss me.
Never mind my bruises,
Hug me, kiss me, suck my juices
Squeez'd from goblin fruits for you,
Goblin pulp and goblin dew.
Eat me, drink me, love me;
Laura, make much of me;
For your sake I have braved the glen
And had to do with goblin merchant men.

GOBLIN MARKET.
CHRISTINA ROSSETTI. 1862

EAT ME,
DRINK ME,
LOVE ME

DAYS, WEEKS, MONTHS, YEARS AFTERWARDS, when we were both wives with children of our own, our mother-hearts beset with fears and bound up in tender lives, I would call the little ones to me and tell them of my early prime, those pleasant days long gone of not-returning time. I would tell them of the haunted glen where I met the wicked goblin men, whose fruits were like honey to my throat but poison in my blood. And I would tell them of my sister, Lizzie, of how she stood in deadly peril to do me good, and won the fiery antidote that cured me of the goblin poison. Then, when my story came to end, I would join my hands to their little hands and bid them cling together, saying, "For there is no friend like a sister in calm or stormy weather; to cheer one on the tedious way, to fetch one if one goes astray, to lift one if one totters down, to strengthen whilst one stands."

And when afterward the children went on their ways to create their imaginary worlds in the afternoon sunlight, or under the shadows of the willow tree at the bottom of the garden, I would weep, silently, from where I sat on my bench, for I had lied in telling them the story in that particular fashion. It was told in that way for their own good, really, with a sound moral embroidered within it, but none of it was true. Except the part about the fruit, and the goblins, and how my sister saved me from a terrible fate.

What I did not tell them was how my sister also destroyed me. A part of me, I should say. Perhaps the best part. But stories for children never hang a broken heart upon the mantel for all to witness and to fear. Instead it is a lively heart, and it is beautiful, isn't it? Thudding away like a fine instrument! The stories one tells children always mean: Life will be happy, my dear ones, even though you will struggle within the world's fierce embrace.

PERHAPS I SHOULD BEGIN WITH the day when everything truly went awry, the day Lizzie and I were walking down by the brook near our family's farm on the outskirts of town, arguing, as we had been doing for much of that summer, and I first came to spot the goblin merchants as they erected their marketplace in the glen across the water. At the time I did not know it was a market they had set themselves to making in such a hidden place, outside of town, where the idea of patrons lining up to buy their goods was an unlikely gamble; but I could hear their voices float toward us, and when I looked over the swaying reeds by the gently flowing water, I could see their tables laden with fruit so lushly colored it shined like precious gems beneath the waning red sun.

It was their faces, though, that charmed me more than anything. Some wore the features of a red fox with sharp ears, charcoal-tipped. Others had long white whiskers that drooped, like a cat who has just lapped a satisfying bowl of cream. One bore the snout of a pig, another peered through the round golden eyes of an insect. Before I could realize what I was doing, I had stopped my progress on the path and Lizzie, who now stood a few steps ahead of me, had turned back to say, "What is it, Laura? Why must you always allow your heart to flap as if it does not belong to you but is possessed instead by the wind?"

I wanted to laugh, and laugh I do now, when I think of Lizzie's frustration over my displays of emotion. After all, we had been arguing that day about how it had been she who had stirred my emotions like a spoon of milk into a cup of tea. "How can you now wish that I not be stirred after having stirred me?" I had asked, just before I heard the goblin voices. But Lizzie had only shaken her head with disgust and refused to answer.

"What is it, Laura?" she asked again, with more concern this time, as I stood on the path by the river, entranced as if in a waking dream.

"Over there," I said, lifting my chin in the direction of the goblin merchants as they set about their queer business. Now they had begun to play music, a bow on a fiddle, with a long reed pipe settled upon the lips of a rat-faced goblin, and as their notes weaved toward us, the other goblins began to dance, arm in arm, with sweat on their brows, circling one another, switching partners.

"They're horrid," said Lizzie. "Do not look at them, Laura. Come. Let us be on our way."

On our way. I looked at Lizzie, who stood half-turned to me, half-turned in the direction of home, and blinked. It was not *our* way. It was *her* way. It had been her way for the entirety of the summer. It had been her way since she first kissed me in late spring, when everything was in riotous flower. It was she who held me close in our bed and told me not to say a word of this to her father, for it would break his heart to know his daughter and his oldest friend's child had been so twisted from what should have been a sisterly bond, as they had raised me in my parents' stead these last few years since my mother and father had died from consumption. It had been Lizzie who said, "We must never tell anyone what we have done, and we must stop ourselves from doing it ever again, Laura."

"But why?" I asked. "It does not feel twisted, as you name it, Lizzie. Is it not love we are feeling?"

"My father would not call it love," said Lizzie. "And if your mother and father were still here instead of with the angels, they would not call it love either."

"What do *you* call it?" I had whispered in the dark of our room, my hand resting near hers, my fingertips barely brushing her tender wrist.

But Lizzie would not answer. She simply turned her back to me, as she did now on the path, turning to lead us the rest of the way home.

"No," I whispered, and turned toward the music instead, turned toward the goblins and the fruits they had assembled upon their tables under the trees in the glen. "This is my way," I said, and stepped off the path to join them.

Behind me, Lizzie gasped. I could imagine her hand, too, delicately flying to cover her mouth as it did whenever she was shocked or frightened. "Laura!" she said, but I continued on my way. At the edge of the brook, I took off my shoes, parted the reeds with my hands, and stepped down into the water. It was ever so cold, but on a day as hot as that one had been—both from the sun and from the strong words we'd exchanged—I welcomed the shiver.

The water rose no higher than my knees, and it took only nine or ten strides before I had reached the other side and could release my dress, which I had bunched within my fists as I crossed over. Immediately, as I came to stand on the other side of the brook, the goblin's music came to an abrupt halt, and they all turned in unison to stare at me.

At first I worried they would not welcome my intrusion, so I began to apologize profusely for interrupting, but even as I unrolled my pleas for forgiveness like a long scroll before their strange faces, the cat-whiskered goblin man lifted his palm and said, "My lady, no apologies! You are our first patron of the evening, and you are welcome to our party. Come, look at our fruits, so succulent, and so deliciously dripping with juices! You will not find such fruits sold in any town. Will you try a pear or an apple or a melon? Won't you taste this peach?"

He produced a perfectly golden peach in his hand, and stretched it across the space between us. At first, he had seemed to be standing too far away to reach me, but in the next moment he stood inches before me, the peach already lifted halfway to my mouth. I could smell its ripeness, and my mouth watered, hungering for its juices.

"I have no money to buy your fruit, sir," I said, turning my face to the ground to hide my embarrassment. Here I had come in order to hurt

Lizzie, here I had come to join the goblin festivities, and yet I was not prepared to purchase their goods at all.

The cat-whiskered goblin's fingertips found my chin, and lifted ever so gently, so that I stared up into his yellow-green eyes, which seemed to sparkle in the fading light, and in that moment I saw that his whiskers and his fur were no more than a mask he had placed upon his face. "You need no money here, my lady," he said. "That is the currency of humans."

"Are you not human, then?" I asked, and could not help but hear a quiver enter my voice.

The cat-masked goblin shrugged, pursing his lips as if he'd tasted something sour. "I have not lived as those in towns live for a long time now, and I do not miss their ways. They are ever so proper, don't you think? And ever so dull-witted with their cordial and celebrated proprietary agreements."

He sighed, grinning with only one corner of his mouth as he removed his fingertips from my chin, and offered me the peach again. "I would take a lock of your hair as payment," he said, almost breathless. "No coin could contain the value of the gold in those locks."

I blushed, for more reasons than I would have liked to. I blushed because he had found a way into my center, into the soft and tender part of me that wished others to see me as valuable, as something beautiful, as something that could not be ignored or forgotten as Lizzie ignored and forgot me. And I blushed because I had let him see my weakness. No woman who sets her sights on a better life should be so visibly vulnerable, yet there I was, blushing as though I were worth nothing.

A tear fell from my eye as I stood there. He caught it on the edge of his finger, then lifted it to his lips to sip at it.

"Exquisite," he said, after swallowing the tear in a theatrical gesture, and I laughed a little in nervousness, but his eyes never strayed from mine during our entire exchange. Not even when he put out his hand to offer me a pair of scissors, and said, "One lock, my dear, and you may join us."

I took the cold metal in my hands and lifted it to my head, pinched a long strand between thumb and forefinger, then slid the blades of the scissors closed. The lock shorn, I dropped it into his outstretched palm, and he closed his hand upon it.

"Your peach, fair maiden," he said, and then placed the fruit into my palm. He held my hand between his own for a long moment, lingering, still holding my gaze steady. Eventually he lifted my hand, and the fruit with it, up to my mouth for me.

I hesitated, but then opened my mouth to take the fruit between my teeth, and when I bit through the downy skin, juice sweeter than any honey from the rock, juice stronger than any man-rejoicing wine, juice clearer than any water flowed into me. Within a moment I was dizzy, but I could not resist the taste, and so sucked and sucked and sucked at the peach, until only its wrinkled pit remained, which I let fall to the ground as I turned toward the cat-masked goblin man's table, to pluck up another and another and another of his fruits, sucking and tearing at the flesh, swallowing as if my life depended upon it, and could not tell night from day any longer, as strange lights filtered through the canopy of the trees, spreading leafy shadows across the masked faces, and the goblins again struck up their music and began to dance around the glen.

One took me by the arm and twirled me into the center of them, where yet another took me up and I gasped to see her long yellow hair and soft round lips before me, the rise of her breasts beneath her tunic. We danced and danced and danced, she and I, spinning and twirling until I could no longer see anything but her face, until I was spun out of the circle like a whirlwind, and only by chance did I catch hold of a tree trunk, where I braced myself against its sturdy body and breathed heavily for a long time while the fireflies fired their bodies around me.

The female goblin left the dancing circles when she noticed I had not been able to continue twirling, and came to find me at my steady tree, still gathering my wits, as if I had just awoken from a deep dream.

"More fruit?" she asked, switching the tail she wore on her bottom back and forth. "I have fruit of my own you have not yet tasted, mistress."

She leaned down and placed her lips upon mine, and sucked at my flesh as I had sucked at the flesh of the fruits. I nearly fell into her arms as she took me into her mouth—I felt myself collapsing a little more with each kiss—but I managed to pull away before she stole my last breath from me.

"I must be going," I said, wiping my lips clean of her, blinking, in shock a little. Beneath the white moonlight, the smear of juice I had wiped away glistened on the back of my hand.

"So early?" the female goblin said, raising one sharply angled eyebrow. "But the moon has just now risen."

"My sister Lizzie," I said. And as soon as her name left my mouth, I began to remember myself, to recollect the argument Lizzie and I had had that afternoon, to remember my love for her, the love she said no one would call love should they ever discover it.

"You may find other sisters here, if you join us," the goblin woman said, trailing a fingertip down my cheek.

"But that is not love," I said, as if I knew what love was wholly from my feelings for Lizzie, as if that were the only love that could ever be.

"Love," the female goblin whispered. She smiled with what might have been sympathy, had I been able to see her entire face behind the mask and know what the rest of her features might tell me. A mask, I thought, was perhaps what I had needed when facing the cat-whiskered man. A mask would have hidden my weakness. "Love," the female goblin said, "comes in many different shapes, my dear. Why approve of only one? Particularly when no one else would approve of the shape of your love anyway?"

I stood, trembling, wishing for an answer, but her question pierced my reasoning through and through.

I turned quickly, and began to run, taken over by a fear that grew in me like a dark tide. I had come to the brink of something. A great chasm of darkness lay before me in the glen, an uncertainty that invited one to throw oneself into it, to lose my self, if I so wanted. But I ran from the sight of it, ran to rejoin the world I knew, regardless of its limitations.

Behind me, the goblin woman shouted, "Do not forget us!" But I did not look over my shoulder or give her a word in return, and only once did I stop to pick up the hard pit of a peach I had dropped earlier that evening, the first fruit I had tasted, which in the momentary madness of my fleeing

I thought I might plant and grow into a tree of my own, to have that fruit available to me forever.

Lizzie. Oh how Lizzie will hate me for what I've done, I thought as I crossed the brook and took the path home. And I was right. As I approached the gate, she was already there, waiting for me with her arms folded beneath her breasts, her form a daunting silhouette in the silver moonlight, a guardian spirit to her father's cottage.

"Laura," she said, shaking her head, her voice filled with what seemed like loathing for me. "Do you know what time it is? Do you know how worried you've made my father and mother? Do you not care what others might think? Don't you remember Jeannie, after all, and what happened to her? The fate she suffered for going into the night?"

I put my head down, shamed, and began to tear up a little. Jeannie. Of course. Jeannie. I had forgotten about Jeannie, young Jeannie, who had gone off one night with a dark-skinned young man who they said lived in the woods, and had returned home some days later, a broken woman. The lovely, poor, ruined Jeannie, who withered like a plucked flower until she died from either heartbreak or, as I secretly believed, from the coldness she was forced to endure from others after returning from the woods. This was what concerned Lizzie, then. What others thought of her.

"It was not as you think," I murmured, preparing to explain myself. But Lizzie's sharp voice rose up again, barring me from speaking.

"I will not hear any of it, thank you very much," she whispered, shrill, in the late summer night air. "Do not speak a word. And do not return to the glen again, Laura, ever, or you will not be able to live here thereafter."

I nodded and wiped my face with the back of my hand, wishing Lizzie might take my tears upon her finger as the cat-whiskered goblin man had done and relieve me of my regret and sorrow, wishing she would at least be kinder.

After my acquiescence, though, she only turned and went into the cottage without another word.

WHAT WOULD I HAVE DONE without Lizzie and her parents? I would have been an orphan in some other house, I'm sure. I might have been given over to an innkeeper and his wife, or I might have been placed as a worker in a factory, at the ripe age of sixteen, when my own parents fell ill and began to pass away before my eyes. Instead, Lizzie's father promised my father, his oldest friend, a friend he called brother, that I would not fall into the hands of strangers and be left alone in the world to fend for myself.

And yet there I was, latching the gate to their cottage behind me, alone, and latching the door of the cottage behind me, alone, and creeping over the creaking floorboards until I could latch Lizzie's and my bedroom door behind me, as if I were a stranger stealing through their property in the middle of the night. Lizzie had already put on her bedclothes and pulled the covers up to her chin. She lay with her yellow hair streaming out on the pillow like an aura of light, her body curled into itself in the same way babies are born into the world. I changed my own clothes and slid into bed beside her, felt the heat of her body warming her half of the bed, and nearly put my hand upon her waist as I had grown used to doing all that spring and summer, before Lizzie grew afraid of our passion and told me it must end or we would burn in hell like poor Jeannie, upon whose grave no grass would grow. I had once planted daisies for poor Jeannie, who everyone shook their heads about whenever her name was mentioned, but no blossoms ever came to bloom. Everything wilted and withered, as Jeannie herself had wilted and withered after she returned from the woods without her dark-skinned suitor.

"Are you awake?" I whispered into the dark that separated us.

Lizzie groaned and told me to be quiet.

"You shall see," I told her. "Tomorrow, I will bring you the most delicious fruit—peaches, melons, fresh plums still on their mother twigs, and cherries worth getting—and then you will no longer feel such anger with me."

Golden head by golden head, we lay in the curtained bed, like two pigeons in one nest, like two blossoms on one stem, like two flakes of newly fallen snow, like two wands of ivory, tipped with gold for awful kings, and heard nothing more from the night but the sound of our own hearts beating, and fell asleep without having reconciled.

❧

EARLY IN THE MORNING, WHEN the first cock crowed, we rose together and, sweet like bees, began our work for the day, neat and busy. We fetched in honey from the combs, milked the cows, flung open the shutters to air the house, and set to rights all that had fallen out of place the day before. With Lizzie's mother, we kneaded cakes of whitest wheat, churned butter, whipped up cream, and then went on our way to feed the chickens before, in the late afternoon, we broke from our duties to sit and sew together for a while, and talk a little about nothing of importance, as we used to do, as modest maidens should, which I could see from the placid smile on Lizzie's face, bent over her needlework, gladdened her. But no matter what we did that day, my thoughts were with the night to come, with the fruits my teeth would meet in, with the music and the dancing, and the goblin men and women who would spin me within their embrace.

When at length the evening reached us, Lizzie and I took up our pitchers to fetch water from the reedy brook, and did not speak of goblins or of fruit, but went along peacefully, as we did at the end of each day. Kneeling by the brook, we dipped our pitchers into the water to fill them with the brook's rippling purple and rich golden flags, and when we stood again, the crags of a nearby mountain were flushed red with the setting sun.

"Come, Laura," Lizzie said. "The day is ending. Not another maiden lags. The beasts and birds are all fast asleep, and soon too shall we be."

I loitered by the reeds, listening for the sound of their voices, waiting to hear a bow eek a tune from the strings of a violin, or a first rush of breath fill the pipes and bring the glen alive with music. "It's early still," I said. "The dew is not yet on the grass, no chill has settled into the wind."

Lizzie, though, was not having any of my excuses. "It's them you're waiting for," she said, "isn't it?"

I turned to face her, and said, "Yes," and said, "If you but tasted their fruit, you would understand me as you once did."

"Then why do you wait?" Lizzie said. "Go to them. They are there, after all, calling for us to join them. *Come buy, come buy!* It is an ugly sort of commerce, Laura. I don't know what you are thinking."

"Wait?" I said. "I wait to hear those voices. You hear them?"

"Yes," Lizzie said, and lifted her chin to gesture toward the glen across the flowing water. "They are there already, waiting for you to return to them."

I nearly spun on my feet like a top to look where Lizzie gestured, but when I faced the glen, I saw nothing but the empty pasture where I had danced and eaten the night before. I heard nothing but the sound of the brook flowing by me. "Where, Lizzie?" I asked. "I see nothing, I hear nothing."

"Good, then!" Lizzie said with a glee that angered me. "Come home with me. The stars rise, the moon bends her arc, each glowworm winks her spark. Let us get home before the night grows dark, for clouds may gather though this is summer weather, put out the lights and drench us."

I stood still as stone and felt cold as stone through and through. "Really, sister?" I said, my eyes wide with fear. "Do you hear them truly, or are you trying to hurt me?"

"*Come buy, come buy!*" Lizzie said again, mocking their voices, making them sound like terrible creatures. "It is good that you cannot hear them," she said. "It means your heart is still your own."

She held her hand out then and curled her fingers inward. "Come, Laura," she said. "Let us be home again."

I did not want to take her hand—I wanted to take the hand of the goblins whose voices I could no longer hear, whose masked faces I could no longer see—but in the end it was the hand offered me, and it was the hand I took.

We went to bed that night and curled around each other as we used to, and for a while I thought that I was better off for not hearing the voices of goblins. But before our twistings and turnings could reach a satisfactory moment, I felt all passion leave me, like a cork released from its bottle, and lay in the dark, wondering about the strange people who had shown me a glimpse of a life I would now never know. Lizzie patted her kisses upon my cheek, upon my shoulders, and stroked my side and waist with her nimble fingers, but the fingers I had longed for in the past few weeks when she had kept them from me, those fingers and their touch no longer held me in the spell they once cast over me.

When Lizzie finally fell asleep, I sat up and looked out the window at the moon hanging low, caught up in the branches of a tree. I cried, silently, and gnashed my teeth like a starved animal, and held the howls of yearning inside my body so Lizzie would not wake and ask me what was the matter.

She should have known. She'd been the matter. Now it was something else taken from me.

❦

FOR DAYS, WEEKS, MONTHS AFTERWARD, I waited in the sullen silence that accompanies exceeding pain, hungering for another glimpse, wanting the sound of their music to find me, eager for the taste of their fruit upon my lips, desiring only to dance within their circle once more. But I never spied the goblin merchants again. Instead, I began to wither, the way Lizzie had warned me poor Jeannie had after returning from the woods without her young man. And as I withered, Lizzie seemed to grow brighter, as if she held a warm fire within her.

In all the months that passed, I had only one brief period of hope, which came when spring returned to us and I recalled the peach stone I had brought home from the goblin revels. I had placed it in a drawer and, upon remembering it, I quickly took it out to set it on a wall that faced south, and soaked it with my tears, hoping it would take root, or grow a green shoot after I planted it in the garden. No shoot ever came, though I dreamed of melons and trees full of ripe apples; and sometimes, as I came to see if the peach kernel was growing, I would be deluded by visions of ripe berry bushes, the way a thirsty traveler in the desert will see water where no water flows.

No more did I sweep the house, no more did I tend to the fowl or cows. No more did I join Lizzie and her mother to knead cakes of wheat, no more did I gather honey. Instead, I sat in the nook by the chimney and nursed my sorrow. And never did I fetch water from the brook, for going there reminded me too much of what I could no longer see, hear, touch, taste.

"Poor Laura," Lizzie said one day in late spring, while I was at my worst. I had stopped eating, because no food set before me tasted of life, and even when I tried to eat for the sake of Lizzie and her parents, I could not take more than two bites before my stomach turned and revolted. "Poor Laura," said Lizzie, coming to sit beside me. She lifted my cold hand from my lap and held it between her burning palms. "I cannot stand to see you suffering like this, sister. Tonight I will put a penny in my purse and go to the goblin merchants for you."

I was too feeble in mind and in body to say anything to stop her, and could only watch as she slid the coin into her purse and went on her daily mission to fetch water from the brook.

What occurred down there, in the glen near the flowing water, beneath the newly leafed trees and the shadows they cast upon the ground beneath them, I could only imagine from my own experiences. But Lizzie was a smart girl, and always prepared to get what she wanted without giving herself over in return. So later, when she returned at moonrise, and spilled into our room, slathered in the juice of goblin fruit from top to bottom, I could not believe the words she sang out to me.

"Laura, oh Laura, did you miss me? Come and kiss me. Never mind my bruises, hug me, kiss me, suck my juices, squeezed from goblin fruits for you. But I did not let them touch me, only you. Only you. Come, Laura. Eat me, drink me, love me. Make much of me. For you I have braved the glen and had to do with goblin merchant men."

With a start I leaped from my chair, already concerned that Lizzie had tasted fruit that would destroy her. I clutched at her, and kissed her, and held her to me, as we once did with great passion. Tears sprang from my eyes, burning as they fell from me. And as the juice from the goblin fruit smeared upon my sister's body filled my mouth, I felt my youth and vigor being restored to me, and tore at my robe, and then at Lizzie's, and we tumbled toward our bed like two awkward dancers, parting the curtains as we fell onto the pillows, and then began to touch each other as we were meant to.

Life out of death. That long night, after we had made love as we used to, I slept with the peace I once knew in life. The shades of gray that had colored me for months began to fade, and in the morning when I awoke, it was as if from a nightmare that I returned to the world, where color and scent and the feeling of Lizzie's skin as I stroked her bare, cream-colored shoulder had returned as well.

When Lizzie rose from sleep as my touch lingered, she yawned, then smiled, and quickly slipped out of bed to dress herself. "Honey, then butter, then the chickens, then the house," she murmured, grinning to herself as she sat in a chair and laced her bodice.

"And after the house," I said, sitting up on one elbow, "the brook. And after the brook, here again, beneath these curtains, where I wish we could stay forever."

Lizzie's grin turned sour the moment I said those words, though. She lifted her face to me and said, "Laura, it was for you that I did that. It was to save you. But it cannot be more. It cannot be what you are thinking. It cannot go on like that between us forever. I will be married one day. I will have children. So, too, will you, if you know what's best for you. But clearly you do not, or we would never have found ourselves in this predicament to begin with."

And at that she rose from her chair and left me there, alone.

IT WAS LIKE A CURSE she threw upon me with those last statements, for as the days and months began to grind beneath my feet, it all came to be true. Lizzie married a young man from a farm just down the way, past the glen; and some time later, after I fully realized we would not be together as I wished, I married too. He was a sweet man, a blacksmith with a sharp black beard and kind blue eyes, and with him I had two children, a boy and a girl to match Lizzie's pair. He was not long for this world, though. A spark flew up one day and blinded him in one eye, and soon the skin there turned an awful red, and then began to fester. The doctor said there was nothing to be done but to help ease him out of this world with the least amount of pain possible, which we did.

Lizzie helped me during that trying time. She came daily with bread and milk and honey, and cleaned my house for me, to save me the work while I tended to my husband. His passing was slow at first, and then he ran toward his end very quickly.

The house and his hearth were sold afterward. I went to live again in the house where Lizzie's parents had once raised us. They were gone by then, too, and Lizzie said it would be better if my children and I were closer, so she could look in on me more often.

She'd bring her own children with her, to play with my Tom and Lily, and we would sew together and try not to speak of the past. Only the present, only daily items and routines would be topics. Any hint of love long past, of passion hidden for the sake of others, and Lizzie would gather up her things and leave.

Sometimes she'd bring her children over and ask me to look after them when she needed to go into town for something. It was during those times that I would tell them the story of the goblin glen, about how my sister had stood in deadly peril to do me good, to save me from an awful fate. The children would listen, rapt and eager to hear the parts about the goblins, and about the fruits, and the music, and the dancing. And afterward they'd run off to play under the shadows of the weeping willow at the bottom of the garden, where once I tried to plant a peach stone out of desperation.

After they were off on their own, I would weep, silently, for having lied to them. The entire tale I told was true, yet none of it was honest. But the stories one tells children always mean: Life will be happy, my dear ones, even though you will struggle within the world's fierce embrace.

When they grow older, I decided long ago—as the days, months, and years come to pass—I will tell them a different story. A story with a good moral of its own to benefit them when they are ready. I will tell them everything they need to know about this world to find or make their happy endings. And if the world cannot provide them with the love they require for happiness, I will tell them to leave it, to join another if one is ever offered. I will tell them to not go back up the path to what they already know. Eat, drink, love without caution. Within this world's fierce embrace, they need not struggle so.

I was coming home from some
place at the end of the world,
about three o'clock of a black winter morning,
and my way lay through a part of town where
there was literally nothing to be seen but
lamps. Street after street, and all the folks
asleep—street after street, all lighted up as if for
a procession and all as empty as a church—till at last
I got into that state of mind when a man listens and listens
and begins to long for the sight of a policeman. All at once,
I saw two figures: one a little man who was stumping along
eastward at a good walk, and the other a girl of maybe eight
or ten who was running as hard as she was able down a cross
street. Well, sir, the two ran into one another naturally enough
at the corner; and then came the horrible part of the thing; for
the man trampled calmly over the child's body and left
her screaming on the ground. It sounds nothing to
hear, but it was hellish to see. It wasn't like a man;
it was like some damned Juggernaut.

THE STRANGE CASE OF
DR. JEKYLL AND MR. HYDE.
ROBERT LOUIS STEVENSON,
1886

THE
TRAMPLING

It starts with a small child—a girl of no more than eight or nine, with stringy blond hair and grease caked under her ragged fingernails—trotting down a street in a not so fashionable district of London. It's 1886. It's nearly three in the morning, the night shrouded in fog. She's barefoot and hungry, and back in the rooms she left just ten minutes ago, her parents have begun making up from the row they've just ended, a row that included a vast amount of cursing, thrown cutlery, and fisticuffs, leaving the girl's mother with a great weal across her cheek and another across her forehead. The girl's been sent for a doctor, who might stitch up the cuts. Her parents' making-up will consist mainly of the girl's father forcing himself into her mother, disregarding the tears in her eyes and the whimpering he mistakes for her pleasure, and in this way he will allow himself to believe that everything that came before that moment has been forgiven.

The girl, as mentioned, is hungry. And also somewhat frightened by the goings-on back home, though over the years her fear of her father's temper and her mother's sharp tongue has waned. Little by little, the girl has come to see that, though one might easily and consistently be hurt in mind or body by living in the circumstances she's been born to, one can survive if one keeps her wits about her. So when a fight breaks out, she knows to slip out the door and wait beneath the window ledge with the flowerless flower box sitting upon it, until the shouting and the tussling is finally over. Which is what she's done. Then her father called her in and said, "Run and get the doctor." Which is what she's doing.

Even this late at night, there are doctors of a certain type— apothecaries more than anything—that will waken and go to someone's aid, even though the streets have almost emptied. Even this late at night, too, you can sometimes find a gentleman who may stop to give a barefoot urchin a coin, enough to buy a sweet from the shops in the morning if she can hide it long enough from her parents. And many gentlemen won't even require her to sing a song or to perform a dance or to allow his hand to caress her for several moments. No, the ideal gentleman will simply press a coin into her hand and will then move along, shaking his head, disturbed by the overwhelming force of pity she's stirred in him. If she can find an ideal gentleman while running for the doctor, she thinks it could at least mitigate some of the disaster she's just lived through.

To find a doctor, she's had to go down a street that she'd probably recognize more easily during the day, when people are actually walking about and the shops are open. She's unsure of whether or not she's taken a wrong turn, because it feels like it's taking longer than usual to find the building where the old sawbones who usually sees to her mother's ailments lives. And despite her belief that there are always kind gentlemen available at any hour, none seem to be appearing now to help her.

The moon is high. The gaslights flicker in the white fog like faraway lighthouse beacons.

Though the girl doesn't see any gentlemen appearing in her path, someone is in fact coming toward her. Someone—or something—is approaching from nearly two blocks away, heading in her direction, his footfalls thudding against the cobblestones, his breathing fast and heavy. He is not a gentleman in the least, though. He is more like some kind of elemental force: a dark wind blowing down an alleyway, pushing over carts, spilling apples, shaking windows until they shatter in his wake. He is hurrying away from something at this moment, his arms pumping furiously, as though he's being chased, and his bloodshot eyes are glistening. When he turns a corner, he sees the little girl just up ahead. She's standing under the foggy glow of a street lantern, a sole actor illuminated by stage lights. He doesn't slow down in the least though. He goes forward, possibly even faster, as if she is just another obstacle placed in his way—an old barrel, or a bin full of rotting cabbages—that for obscure and paranoiac reasons he must now confront.

The girl turns to see him barreling down on her, coming at her with the pace and intent of a juggernaut, and promptly she opens her mouth to scream. Before she can loose a cry though, he is there, knocking her backward, her head hitting the stone upon which she'd been standing, and then he tramples over her, his boots thudding across her small body, snapping her left arm in two.

After which the girl does manage to scream, loudly and over and over, unwittingly calling the attention of someone nearby. A gentleman, actually. An ideal gentleman by the name of Enfield who, on his way home from what he'll later describe to a confidante as some place at the end of the world, has just witnessed what's occurred from across the street, and who now shouts, "You there! You, sir! I say. Halt!"

When the dark wind that blew the girl over does not heed his words, Enfield rushes across the street and begins to chase the monster.

It is a long chase, though Enfield does not feel exactly how long it is as adrenaline pumps through his body. As the cries of the little girl rise like frightened night birds, he quickens his pace, faster and faster, going one block, two, three, then a fourth, until suddenly he is breathing down the neck of the man who assaulted her, grabbing the collar of his overcoat, and lifting him off the ground by an inch. "I said to stop!" Enfield shouts, and then places the offensive cur back on his feet, only for the man to turn around to reveal his face, shadowed beneath the brim of his hat.

It is a normal enough face, but something in it strikes to the heart of Enfield, sending a shiver through his body, weakening his grip on the man's collar. It is a normal enough face—two eyes, not set too far apart or too close, two ears in proper alignment, a nose without a break, a mouth full of all its teeth even—but something in how it is all put together signals pure evil. The evil man sneers, and Enfield says, "You, sir, have hurt a child. A child to whom we shall now give our help."

No argument ensues. The horrid little man—who is actually not little so much as stooped over as he walks—simply says, "Very well, then," and walks alongside Enfield, who has still not released his grip on the man's collar. It's only after they walk the four blocks back to the street corner where the terrible incident occurred that Enfield realizes the length of the chase and begins to feel winded as he returns to normal.

A small crowd has gathered around the girl at this point: her parents have come looking for her, along with the doctor she'd intended to find in the first place, and a few people from the neighborhood that were woken by her cries. Her mother's face is shrouded with a shawl she's pulled over her head, as though she means to keep out the winter chill instead of hiding the violence done to her earlier that evening. Her father still stinks of gin, but by now he's at least able to stand without wobbling. The little girl looks up at them all as they converse above her.

After examining her briefly, the old sawbones snaps his black bag closed and stands again, telling everyone, "Her arm is broken, I'm afraid," which sends them all into a concerted argument with the man who ran her over.

They have questions for him. What is his name? "Hyde," he tells them. Her mother repeats that name like a curse, then spits at the man's feet, mere inches from the girl's body. They will bring that name to ruin, they tell him. They will make such a scandal of that name that it will stink from one end of London to the other.

The man who trampled the girl cannot seem to make a face that exudes any hint of an apology, which angers the gathered crowd even more. He wears a continual sneer, as though all of humanity is beneath his contempt, as if all of humanity is his for the trampling. He adjusts the brim of his hat so that it shades his eyes into dark pools, and says, "If you choose to make capital out of this accident, I am naturally helpless. No gentleman but wishes to avoid a scene. Name your figure."

Numbers fly back and forth over the girl's head. They seem to have forgotten her at this point. The man, Enfield, who brought her assailant back to face justice, says, "One hundred pounds!" and the girl's father looks at him as though he's demanded the moon itself.

"A hundred pounds!" says Hyde. "Why, that is enough to purchase a house!"

"Or to purchase our silence," Enfield says, his voice low, almost growling like a dog giving warning.

"Very well, then," says Hyde. "A hundred pounds."

"And how will you produce a hundred pounds at this hour?" Enfield asks, seeming angry that Hyde has agreed to meet his figure, as if he were hoping the man would argue, so that he might instead have him thrown into prison.

Hyde simply grins an evil grin and says, "Follow me."

Before they leave, the old sawbones sets the girl's arm and arranges it in a sling, muttering, "It's a simple break, but do not let her move it." He also gives the girl's mother a vial to help the girl sleep, if sleep will not come tonight. "Only a thimbleful, though," he advises. "It is strong stuff." Then the girl's father lifts her up and places her into her mother's arms.

The mother takes the girl back to their dirty little rooms and puts her to bed, then sits beside the girl's cot to sing her a lullaby. Her notes flicker like the flame in the bedside lantern as she sings an old song about a child who's been ill and, after breathing her last breath, is released from her body to walk across a star-filled sky. Afterward, the girl pretends to fall asleep, and the mother folds her arms across her stomach as she rocks back and forth in her chair, over and over, stifling her sobbing. The girl lies in bed, eyes closed, pretending to sleep so that the mother will eventually stop crying and leave her altogether.

It is only after the mother stands to go, closing the door behind her, that the girl's eyes fly open again, and she stairs up at the ceiling, where shadows are starting to gather. They move as if they have a life of their own, bending and winking. She watches them shift and transform in a hypnotic fashion, until suddenly she sees a figure forming above her, and she begins to scream.

❦

WE'LL LEAVE THE GIRL LIKE that for a moment. We must now follow the men—her father, the old sawbones, and Mr. Enfield, her savior—on their journey to acquire Mr. Hyde's hush money.

Mr. Hyde leads them away from the scene of the crime, stamping his cane on the stones in front of him. They walk not a great distance, but in that short span the streets change into a somewhat dingy neighborhood. Dingy, but what one calls quiet. Dignified working class quarters, where the houses are bland but livable, and where the streets during the daytime take on a friendlier air as the shopkeepers push their grains and goods outside for passersby to consider. This neighborhood borders a much better one, so those who live on this particular street take pride in their nearness to polite society.

They come to a stop at one particularly sinister-looking block of building—two stories high with not even one window, and a gable that thrusts itself out and over them like a gargoyle—and there Hyde opens a recessed door with a key and looks over his shoulder to say, "One moment, I will be right back," before closing the door behind him.

The door is a blistered and discolored affair, set back into a sliver of darkness. It's the sort of place where tramps take cover, sleep, and strike matches against the panels. It's the sort of place where children decide to keep shop, where schoolboys try their knives on the mouldings. Enfield, the father, and the old sawbones look upon it and shiver.

Hyde returns quickly, as promised, and hands the father coins and a check. "What's all this?" the father asks, and Hyde explains that he only has ten pounds in his quarters, and the rest can be withdrawn from the banks in the morning. Before the father can say anything, Enfield takes the check from him and examines it for a long moment, after which he lowers it slowly, so that Hyde sees the man's eyes revealed little by little, and then his entire face. And Enfield's face betrays a shocking disbelief.

"How did you come by this check, sir?" Enfield inquires calmly, though his voice is tinged with an even greater edge than before. And Hyde does not attempt to answer with any complex lie. He simply assures Enfield that the check, despite being signed by a Dr. Henry Jekyll, is quite good.

"If it is good," Enfield says, "then you wouldn't mind waiting with the rest of us until morning, when we could all go to the bank together." He looks at the father, who nods, and then at the old sawbones, who sighs but also nods, and then turns back to Hyde, who is grinning beneath the shadow of his hat's brim.

"But of course," says Hyde. "Where, however, might we wait?" He looks back to the sinister building behind him, and the other men look with him. Hyde's grin grows wider, though they can't see it. And their own faces look grim as they consider what Hyde's lair might contain.

"My rooms are not far from here," Enfield says, and they follow him several blocks into the bordering streets, where polite society still sleeps.

They pass two hours in Enfield's drawing room, which has a fire going for warmth, and he shares out a bit of brandy between the men, Hyde included. The father drinks his too quickly, rather than sipping. Enfield is perturbed by the man's lack of manners, but rises to pour him another regardless. If he didn't, he would not be a gentleman. The men do not speak much, and the father eventually falls asleep in a wingback leather chair, snoring a bit as he descends into unconsciousness. Hyde snorts at the irony of this development, and peers through the fire lit shadows to see if Enfield and the old sawbones, too, find it humorous that the father of the victim is the first to reconcile himself with their odd situation enough to sleep soundly in a strange room among strangers, one of whom has injured his daughter. Enfield rolls his eyes a little, then looks toward the window, where the sun has just begun to rise behind the silhouetted roofline across the street, turning the sky pink, then orange, and then finally a blue that glistens like ice.

When the bank opens, the men are already outside, waiting to enter. Waiting to end their enforced company. So they slip through the pillars into the building, where Enfield instructs the father and the old sawbones to wait on a bench near the front, and then he and Hyde continue further, seeming to grow smaller as they approach the center of the high-vaulted room. A man comes out from behind a large desk to greet them, shakes their hands vigorously, takes the check from Enfield, asks for them to wait just a moment, ferries the check to an inner chamber, then returns minutes later with a billfold of bank notes, which he presents to Enfield, which Enfield carries back to the father waiting on the soft-leather bench, to place it in the father's hands gently, soberly, with an air of nobility, as if he is knighting or anointing the father with this money that has purchased their silence.

The check is good, as Hyde said it would be. The father now holds a hundred pounds on his person. More than he has ever seen in his life, even if he added up every shilling that had ever slipped through his grubby fingers.

They stand in a circle staring down at the bank notes, except for Hyde, who is already moving toward the exit. "It has been an interesting evening, my friends," he says, and then he laughs loudly—once, twice, a third time—as he pauses at the door to look over his shoulder briefly, to sneer at them once more. And then he is gone, sticking his cane out before his next step, strolling among the good people of London.

The men dissolve their company and the father returns to his dirty rooms in his dirty district, where the mother has fallen asleep sitting at the kitchen table, her head rested on her folded arms. He wakes her up, laughing, and dances a jig as he shows her the money, which makes the mother laugh as well now, hysterically so, and then she has a kettle on and she's still laughing and laughing—she cannot stop laughing—and they're making plans, so many plans, more plans than the money can even make happen. A house. New wardrobes. Perhaps they will open a shop for the mother. She's a good seamstress, after all. She could have her own place, if they'd purchase the equipment and all of the materials she'd need to make a go of it. Together they could make a go of it, they're thinking, they could make a go of this life that they'd nearly given up on after years and years of backbreaking labor that never amounted to anything but squalor.

The girl, who has not yet fallen asleep, hears them laughing and dancing. She stares up at the ceiling and shakes her head at each idea they produce in the midst of their hysteria. These dreams, she knows, none of them will come true. She knows this because she knows her father, knows his rarely kept promises, knows his seeming inability to flourish even when good fortune befalls him. Whatever he touches turns to dust and ruin, the opposite of Midas.

And she is right. The father will not buy the house they've imagined that morning. He'll rent one for them instead, in a better neighborhood, of course, and yes, he'll buy them new clothes. But the dreamed-of shop for her mother will never come to fruition. He'll have started drinking far too much gin again by then; and really, even now, as they're making plans for what to do with the money, he is already thinking of his next glass. And as the money withers little by little, he will grow frightened and will begin to gamble, trying to regain his losses, but the money will only disappear faster and faster, as if it's caught a wasting disease, and eventually he'll be unable to pay the rent on the new house and will be evicted, only to return to the dirty rooms in which they are now, at this very moment, dancing and laughing and making plans for a better future.

The girl shakes her head as she holds her broken arm and tries not to look up at the shadows crawling on her ceiling. They seem to be alive, to crawl like snakes.

THIS IS THE LAST WE'LL see of the girl in a somewhat hopeful situation. Her arm will heal, of course, but the old sawbones unfortunately did not set it properly, and because of this she will not be able to bring it behind her back or raise it entirely over her head for the rest of her life. It will be a limitation that excludes her from certain kinds of work. Like the work her mother had lined up for her prior to the trampling. Work as a servant in a decent house, where the girl might have taken coats from gentlemen as they entered to visit the girl's hypothetical master, for whom she might have cleaned and blacked the stove and helped the cook with preparations in the kitchen.

Instead, in the coming months, after the father has moved them to the new house, then moved them back to their old rooms after losing the money, the girl will be turned down for the position as it becomes clear she isn't capable of doing certain kinds of labor. Instead, she'll go to work in a match factory at the end of their grubby street, where she will work sixteen-hour shifts dipping matchsticks into vats of phosphorous, the fumes of which will eventually come to rot her teeth. She will continue to dip matchsticks from then on, from age ten until age sixteen, which is when she'll begin to cough blood into her hands and onto her pillow—another effect of the fumes she'll breathe for sixteen hours out of each day of her life, more chemicals than oxygen—and when that happens she will remain in bed for the rest of her remaining days and nights, which are unfortunately quite limited.

Hers is not an unusual life, really, even now, where we stand over a century beyond the girl's desperate circumstances. Cell phones manufactured by indentured factory workers, clothes made in places where sixteen-hour work shifts are still quite ordinary, where such a shift may produce only a dollar or two for those who work them, and where children scavenge among the material wreckage other nations have deposited in their homelands, looking for copper and other metal that might be salvaged. It is not unusual, even now, to hear of places where the powerful have arranged for the working populations to enter into a new kind of slavery, where a person can toil freely, without compulsion, for the profit of others yet still go hungry, still live in squalor despite their hard labor. It is not unusual, even now, to hear stories of the powerful attempting to eradicate laws that have been erected to protect people from allowing misery of this kind to dominate their lives. Laws that would protect people from *them*, really, the Hydes of the world, who appear before us as the highest members of society, seeming as good as Dr. Jekyll himself seemed, doing charity work and throwing galas for the underprivileged in an effort to obscure their all-consuming greed, to help obscure their inner desire to harm, to exploit, to trample.

The girl lies in bed with her hands on her stomach. She hasn't been to the matchstick factory for nearly a week. Her breathing is shallow; her chest stutters as it rises and falls. It is almost time for her to leave her body and walk across the night above the rooftops, to leave the pain this world has given her, as in her mother's song. But for now she still breathes. She still lingers. She still stares up and into the vault of darkness gathering above and waits for the shadow that has haunted her since the night of her trampling. The shadow that had made her scream that night, right before we left her to follow the men to Enfield's quarters.

On that night, the night Hyde ran the girl over, she'd feigned sleep so her mother would leave her bedside. And afterward the girl had opened her eyes, only to see a cloud of black shadows swirling above her. At first the shadows moved like gentle winds, but the longer she watched, the faster they stirred, growing furious and more powerful, bending across her ceiling, until all at once they coalesced into the figure of a man, and in the next moment the man dove toward her.

The mother, from the front room, had heard and came running, casting out the shadowy figure in the very instant she opened the door and filled the room with light from the kitchen. "What is it, love?" she asked the girl. "Is it your arm?"

But the girl only shook her head and said, "It was him. It was him again. That man. He was coming to trample me."

"Oh love," her mother said. "It's all over now. It's all over."

But it wasn't over, not really. Not for the girl, who would continue to see his shadow appear above her every night for the rest of her brief life, even after other horrors she would eventually encounter at the factory might have replaced him as a alternative source of torment. He was still out there. It was not over. Not for anyone. The girl knew this on the night he trampled her, and she knows it still, now, in her final hour. Even as she waits for her last breath to leave her, she can hear the clomping of his heels on the cobblestones and his heavy breathing as he approaches. And then he is there in the room with her once more.

She gasps, releasing a chilled plume of breath into the air above her, and then she is skipping across the night sky above a jagged line of London's rooftops, free, as the lullaby her mother once sang her promised.

He is out there, even now, still running with the pace and intent of a juggernaut down streets and alleyways, prepared to trample over anything and anyone, prepared to trample over the world if he has to, still sneering, as if all of humanity is beneath him.

There comes John's sister.
Such a dear girl as she is, and so
careful of me! I must not let her
find me writing.
She is a perfect and enthusiastic
housekeeper, and hopes for no better profession.
I verily believe she thinks it is the writing
which made me sick!
But I can write when she is out, and see her a long
way off from these windows.
There is one that commands the road, a lovely shaded
winding road, and one that just looks off over the country. A
lovely country, too, full of great elms and velvet meadows.
This wall-paper has a kind of sub-pattern in a different
shade, a particularly irritating one, for you can only see it in
certain lights, and not clearly then.
But in the places where it isn't faded and where
the sun is just so—I can see a strange, provoking,
formless sort of figure, that seems to skulk about
behind that silly and conspicuous front design.
There's sister on the stairs!

THE YELLOW WALLPAPER.
CHARLOTTE PERKINS GILMAN.
1892

THE CREEPING WOMEN

"WHAT A *DELICIOUS* GARDEN!" JANE said after we moved into the house and began to explore the grounds of the estate my brother had leased for the summer.

It was good to hear such joy in Jane's voice, for she tends to be absorbed in melancholy matters most days, and as spending the summer at the estate—three miles away from the nearest village and other people—was for her sake, I was glad to see such an immediate, happy response from her.

It *was* a delicious garden, I must admit, though I'm not sure I would have employed that particular word to describe it. But Jane is (*was?*) a writer. Whenever she talks, she says things in such a peculiar way that I feel as if I can understand whatever she speaks of in a new manner, the way clouds sometimes take on the form of an elephant or a castle, but only once someone else sees them as such do they become apparent to others.

As we strolled along the box-bordered path in the gardens that day, for instance, Jane told me that she sometimes saw expressions in inanimate things. I did not encourage her to continue in this line of thought, of course, as it was the sort of thinking that had concerned my brother John for a good many months, but Jane went on without any prodding on my part.

"I used to lie awake as a child and get more entertainment and terror out of blank walls and plain furniture than most children could find in a toy-store," she told me. She was not looking at me when she said this, but instead had lifted her chin and seemed to peer outward and upward, perhaps at the clouds on the horizon, seeing one of those forms I could not locate before she saw it. But it also somehow seemed as if she were performing for me. That is the thing about Jane, one of her many charming aspects: One can never tell if she truly believes the queer things she proclaims, or if she is just having a bit of fun with you.

"Really, Jane," I replied, offering a friendly but disbelieving grin in return for her childhood confession. I liked Jane so very much. I wanted to be good friends with her, good sisters, but I'd known for a long time, since before my brother had announced their engagement, that I should never allow myself the pleasure of believing, even for a moment, in the romantic nature of Jane's perspective.

"Yes, really," Jane said. She smiled wistfully. She had seen life, she said, where others could see no living creature. "In fact," she continued, "I remember what a kindly wink the knobs of my family's big, old bureau used to have, and there was one chair that always seemed like a strong friend. I could hop into that chair and be protected if ever something frightened me."

I pressed my lips together firmly and did not give her another response. John would have been upset if he felt I had encouraged this sort of talk from Jane when he was, at that very moment, trying to cure her, to return her to her proper self.

But truly! *The winking knobs of a bureau? A chair that is a strong friend?* I will never know how Jane comes up with such ideas.

I shook my head that afternoon, two weeks after we had moved into that ghastly summer estate, as we walked among the flowers, in the shade of the tall oaks, and I shake my head now as I sit here recalling that very moment. I think it is strange, however, to do now as I once did in a memory as I recall it.

That is also the sort of odd observation Jane might have had before she became fixed upon that horrid wallpaper.

I shall not dwell on such thoughts, though. I shall not be like Jane was then.

"The problem with Jane," John would often say, "is that she is endlessly thinking about her own condition."

"There is a forest in that wallpaper, Jennie," Jane told me, only a month ago, in early midsummer. "Can you see it?"

But I would not permit myself to enter into those dark woods. Not after seeing how it seemed we might lose Jane to them forever.

❧

It was Jane who first convinced me to take up the habit of keeping a log of my days as they pass away. I would never have thought to keep a narrative of my own life, but Jane said every woman should tell her own story, lest it be told by someone else. She was quite convincing. Jane was always quite convincing about anything she put her mind to. But it was really her words—the way she used them—that convinced people. And so, properly convinced, I took up ink one day and began to scratch my days into this sheaf of paper.

"A thread," Jane once called it. She meant the line of words on a page. "Look at the way the lines make a pattern, Jennie," she had said, and I watched as the tip of her soft finger traced the curved and ragged edge of her own diary.

Another time, it was not a sewn pattern but a piano. "Look at these thick, white spaces between the paragraphs," she said, "and the winding empty space of the borders. This page looks like the keys of a piano, does it not, Jennie? The black keys between the white spaces? If you play these paragraphs as well as the white spaces between them, I do believe they will also make as much music as a piano."

"Really, Jane," I said, shaking my head, and she put her hand upon my shoulder to squeeze gently, as if I were a child she were teaching.

Heat rushed to my cheeks, and I knew that I could not hide it. Surely my face was pink. I looked away, but Jane took hold of my chin between her thumb and forefinger, then pulled my face back to look at hers.

"Poor Jennie," she said. "Do not be afraid of me. We shall be such good sisters after John and I marry."

"That is my hope," I said, looking down at the page before me, at the paper she'd given me.

"Tell your story, then," said Jane, and she left me there in my room to look at the blankness of those pages alone, pondering what sort of patterns I might make out of the words I had not yet written, wondering what sort of music I might yet compose.

❧

"A HEREDITARY ESTATE," SHE HAD called this place when we first arrived. "A haunted house, surely."

I chuckled at the idea, but John gave me a quick look and I forced my smile away, as I have learned to do from a young age around my brother. John does not entertain superstitions, even in jest. He does not believe in anything that cannot be seen, heard, smelled, tasted, felt. And he requires those who surround him to not utter a word of such things, or else suffer his looks. He has many looks, too, though it is the ugliest of them that he has always reserved for me. To Jane, he gives his kindest looks, the looks of a father who dotes on a young daughter, and finds whatever she does to be pleasing.

Except Jane's writing, of course. That never did please John, even before Jane's nervous depression, her hysteria, became apparent. It was after the melancholia enveloped her that he began to announce what I had always known he privately disliked. It was by his looks, of course, that I perceived his secret. Whenever Jane mentioned her writing, I could see his disdain. For her work. For her thoughts. For her art, I daresay. John's eyes would narrow a little, as if he were wincing from the pain of a sliver suddenly slipped beneath a fingernail, and if he were sitting in a chair, his fingers would begin to tap against the arm, making a rhythm very much like a funeral march.

"A hereditary estate," though, as Jane had declared. Indeed, this place was meant for a different sort of people. John's work as a physician certainly made us comfortable in our family home, but that house! Those rooms! Those gardens! It was all so much. So very, very much.

And yet it was a remote place, stark despite the grandeur of its halls and ballroom, far too neat and orderly despite its rambling stairwells and overgrown gardens, its shattered greenhouses that haunted the meadows nearby. By their looming frames and broken glass, I could see why Jane called it a haunted house, for it is haunted by the gone-away life of its previous inhabitants. Everywhere you look, you will find something chosen by someone else, and if you are inclined, as Jane is, to think about invisible things, you will wonder (as Jane wondered, as I have learned how to wonder from Jane) who it was that selected that chintz-covered chair, that old rocking-horse, this particularly gloom-fogged mirror that stares at me whenever I rise from my writing table to attend to Jane or to some aspect of the house itself.

Or that wallpaper. Jane often wondered aloud who had chosen that wretched yellow wallpaper. She spoke of it so often, in a way that made one feel that, if she could only discover who made that decision, she might undo it like a curse.

❧

JOHN CHOSE WHAT HAD SURELY once been the nursery for Jane's room as soon as we had arrived; though Jane said immediately that she would rather they take a room on the first floor, the one that opened onto a piazza where, beyond the piazza she could see the broken greenhouses that lingered amid the meadows in the distance. "What a lovely thing to see every day," Jane had said, but John only replied that there was only one window in that room and not space for two beds, and no near room for him if she took this one.

I could tell straight away how much Jane disliked the room upstairs. It wasn't even the yellow wallpaper that drew her attention so much all at once, but the bars on the windows and the iron rings in the walls. "This looks as if it were a gymnasium for school children once upon a time," she said, looking around the place with a doubtful eye. There were strips of wallpaper torn away near the headboard, and chunks of plaster dug out of the walls here and there. Gouges in the floor. Really, I don't know what John was thinking. When I looked at Jane's face, I could see the thought that she was forming at that very moment. *Is this where I'm to live for the next three months? In this ghastly room full of the screams of ghostly children?*

The wallpaper she noticed specifically. When her eye landed upon it, her obvious doubt transformed instead to confusion, and she tilted her head as she moved slowly forward to the wall across the room. She lifted one gloved finger in front of her face when she reached the wall, and began to trace the lines of the paper's designs, as if she were studying it. Quickly, though, she snatched her hand back as if a snake had lashed out of the strange design to bite her.

"What is the matter, Jane?" John asked from the doorway.

Jane turned around, her eyes wide, and said, "It *is* horrible wallpaper, isn't it?"

This made John laugh deeply. He folded his hands over his waist, delighted. He did like Jane's wit so much, I grant him that, and I would find even more fault in him if he had not. He nodded but said, "No," they could not tear it down or replace it, because if he let Jane change the wallpaper, it would then be the bedstead, and then it would be removing the bars from the windows, and then the gate from the head of the stairs, and whitewashing the basement, "and dear, we are only leasing the place for three months, Jane, really."

Jane soon took his meaning and nodded in acquiescence.

"Then do let us go downstairs now," she said. "There are such pretty rooms there, don't you think?"

He took her in his arms to lead her away from the nursery, and when they were through the doorway, he stopped to look over his shoulder and say, "Jennie, be a good girl and make up the room for us. And see what we have in the kitchen. I arranged for the pantry to be filled, but I have not the slightest clue what we have been sent."

"Of course," I said, nodding, smiling, my own hands folded over the apron at my waist.

Then John led her out of the room, unlatched the gate that had once kept the children from falling down the staircase, and were gone from my sight.

IN THE EARLY DAYS OF our summer at the estate, I gave Jane a wide berth. John would leave us, it seemed, for days on end, to return to town where he had serious cases to attend. Once, I counted five days gone before John returned. I had heard Jane sobbing behind the door of her room not a half-hour before he appeared on the front lawn. Jane cried often that summer, at various times throughout the day, though she tried her best to hide her tears from me and Mary, who was looking after the baby. And when John climbed the stairs to Jane's room to find her face red and chapped with salt, he grew angry.

"You must use your good sense and will to stop yourself from indulging in needless sorrow, Jane!" he nearly shouted. I had been across the hall, placing folded linens onto a shelf. When I looked over my shoulder, I could see through the doorway as Jane cringed at the sound of his voice. I knew that well, myself. John had always been a loud sort, even when he and I were both children. When he did not get his way, he would grimace at our father, scream like a possessed person at our mother, and when it came to me he did not hesitate to pinch, shove, or hit.

When John was gone, though, Jane would leave her room (where he had advised her to stay as much as possible, "for the good of her health"), and walk the paths through the meadows and gardens. I would stay in the shadows of the oaks that lined the way down to the wharf, and watch her from afar. I did not want to disturb her in these moments, when it was clear she felt better. A calm washed over her face whenever John was gone, when she could walk the perimeter of the estate, or sit beneath the roses on the front porch. And though at times I felt odd for stalking her, for creeping among the shadows of the arbors, I did not want to let Jane out of sight for fear that she might disappear into the water down by the bay.

There were times too, though, that Jane was the one who stayed behind in the house, and I was the one who walked the paths of the gardens. At these times, I would leave her behind to write. She believed her writing to be a secret, but you cannot keep secrets from a housekeeper. Which is what I was. Which is what Jane believed I had no better hopes for as a station in life. I found that in the pages of her days once, but it did not offend me as much as it might have had it been the truth. In fact, as Jane observed in that particular entry, I *was* a seemingly enthusiastic housekeeper. But it was not an enthusiasm rooted in the core of my being. It was for my brother John that I performed that role with dutiful excitement. It was to avoid the moments when he might take me away into a closet and stick his finger in my face, or clutch my throat in his thick hands, squeezing. It was to avoid John's slap against my cheek, the grip on my arm, the yellow and purple bruises he left there, like blossoms.

It is not difficult to seem enthusiastic if the consequences otherwise might mean seeing John's shadow spread across the floor, pooling around my feet, while I folded the laundry.

It did bother me, though, that Jane believed I thought it was her writing that made her sick. That is why I would leave her to indulge in it, allowing her to think it was her secret.

She did not notice me as I stood in shadow, beneath the rose trellis of the porch, looking past those pink and white cups of light, looking through their filter to see her face framed in the window, where she would sit, head bent over her papers, scratching out her days in the cell of a room with the nib of the pen she kept hidden beneath her pillow.

She did not notice me when, sometimes—oftener and oftener—I would see her stand from her chair and place a pale hand against the yellow wallpaper.

❦

SHE HAS A SWEET FACE, Jane. It is soft, curving, and when she has not been crying, her skin holds a faint peach color. Her eyes are blue, like the eyes of a fine doll I had as a child, but her hands do not look delicate at all. She has a thick callus upon her middle finger, which in some lights appears quite red, but only when it is not smirched with ink, which occasionally lingers on her right hand in various places. During this summer at the estate, however, her hand was quite the opposite. It could have been a fine model's hands, long fingered, always clean. You would think she hadn't been writing at all, and in fact she had begun to go days and then weeks without doing so. John approved of this change. He noticed the cleanliness of her writing hand and said, "You have good sense about you, after all, dear Jane," and all the while he held her hand in his own like a kitten, smiling and smiling and smiling.

This was soon after the Fourth of July, after Jane's mother and her sister Nellie came to visit for several days, bringing Nellie's children in tow, like a line of goslings. Between Nellie's children and Jane's own baby, dear thing, being brought out more regularly by Mary to make the rounds of social engagement with grandmother, aunt, and cousins, Jane began to shrink further and further into the background of the household. I found her hiding in other rooms, away from everyone. I found her bedroom door locked on several occasions, and would put the flat of my hand against it, tapping gently, saying, "Jane. Jane, dear, can I help you?" But she would ask me to go away, and so I would.

I had witnessed Jane's decline for the weeks leading up to that visit, but had not reported Jane's odd behaviors to John when he asked about her. Always soon after John returned from several days in town, seeing to his patients, he would take me aside to ask how Jane had been in his absence, and I might have told him a great many things. I might have told him how I had seen Jane lingering by the yellow wallpaper in her nursery room for hours, for instance, or how I had heard Jane sobbing into her pillow at various times of the day. I might have said how I heard Jane muttering to herself when she thought no one was nearby to hear her, or how she would stare out of her window for long stretches of time, like a princess locked in a tower, and how once she asked, "Jennie, do you, too, see the women creeping about in the gardens?"

I had been making up her bed when she asked me that, and though I knew immediately that this was a delusion on Jane's part, I went to the window to stand beside her and look where she was looking. I saw nothing, of course, only the flowers and the thorny bushes and the gnarled old trees of a formerly well-kept garden. Instead of telling Jane what I saw, though, I asked, "What would you say if I said that I did see them?"

Jane turned to face me, her mouth slightly parted, and said, "Oh, Jennie. Then I would say we are both doomed."

I patted her hand, the hand that so often stroked the yellow wallpaper of her nursery, where she had shown me the broken pattern in the design several times over the past few weeks, as if she had forgotten she'd shown me each time prior, and gave it a slight squeeze.

And when John returned to ask a report of her behavior, I said, "She's doing quite well. I should think she's quite capable of returning to her social life at this point."

To which John replied, "I am the physician in this house, Jennie. Do remember your place in the scheme of things."

I nodded, and looked at the floor, folded my hands at my waist. How could I forget?

John got the answers he wanted out of young Mary, however, which did not surprise me. Mary is a lovely girl, but a bit naïve. When John asked her, too, about whether or not the missus had been able to spend time with the baby, Mary said that she had not, and that at any time Mary brought the child near Jane, Jane's face would pale, her eyes would display fright in their widening, and she'd clutch at her neck as if someone had placed a rope around it.

John nodded. I could see him tallying up the signs and symbols. And not a night passed before, at dinner, he broke apart our perfectly ordinary conversation to tell Jane, "If you do not improve more quickly, I'll be taking you to see Weir Mitchell in the autumn."

Jane blanched from the threat of having to see Weir Mitchell, the physician who had devised the very "rest cure" John had elected as Jane's treatment for her hysteria, and she blanched, too, I think, from the embarrassment John had just heaped upon her in front of me. I looked down at my hands, hoping not to call John's attention toward me, and Jane said, "If only you would let me make a visit to Cousin Henry and Julia. I need people, John, and social engagement."

"My dear," said John, "you would not be able to stand it, and you would not be able to especially after you'd arrived. No, I think not. Not until I can see you have better control over your emotions."

Jane then uttered a string of hopeless words at John. If only he would listen to her, she said. If only he could understand what she was saying. But John only shook his head, sighing, pushing his unfinished plate away from him, and eventually Jane began sobbing, as she usually does in private.

John gathered her into his arms then, and carried her upstairs to her room like a new bride, saying, "There, there, my child, my little girl, my goose, you see this is exactly why you cannot manage a visit with anyone."

I retreated to my own room, which shared a wall with Jane's, near her headboard, and listened as John continued his attempt to calm her. He called her his darling and his comfort, he said she was all he had in the world, and that she must take care of herself, that she must make herself well again. Which angered me initially, because John was lying to her. But, really, I couldn't expect him to reveal his secrets. Jane was not the *only* thing he had in the world. He had our family home, left to him by our father who had passed away three years before, he had women he sometimes called his "patients" but who did not suffer from any ailments—several letters had strayed from their path to him on occasion only to land in my own hands, so I know what I am speaking of—and of course, of course he had my own inheritance, which my sick father, long widowed by my mother, had entrusted to his care until the day I married. A condition my father had laid out in his last will, after John convinced him that I had no head for money.

Though I do keep the household budget myself, and there is never a penny lost or overspent.

All that night, John laid by Jane's side, whispering his sweet lies to her, until eventually her whimpers ceased, and then I heard the bed begin to move with John's body atop Jane's. The bed was noisy, and Jane's whimpers eventually returned, and I shut my eyes, clapped my hands against my ears, trying to force the knowledge of their coupling out of my mind. It was a horrid thing to know what he was doing to her. Horrid because of his lies, his infidelities, horrid because of his monstrous possession of both her body and soul. I squirmed in my own bed, shook my head as if he were doing it to me, too, as if he had me in the closet again and then I nearly screamed, but took my hands from my ears and clapped them over my mouth to catch it.

Dear Jane, I thought. *You sweet dove. You deserve so much better than this. If I could, I would share the words I have been writing since you gave me a sheaf of paper and I would play the black and white keys of the paragraphs for you like a song.*

I lulled myself to sleep with images of Jane and I sitting on the front porch among the roses, and did not allow myself to hear any more of their sounds.

In the morning, when I went to check on Jane, she was already awake and dressed, and already standing with her hand placed against the yellow wallpaper. "It has a yellow smell, Jennie," she said. "Don't you think?"

I did not answer her.

"Jennie," she said, "there is a forest in this wallpaper. Can you see it?"

I did. I did see it, finally, the thing Jane had been seeing in the wallpaper. There was a forest in that design, a winding and confusing forest, and a woman hidden—no, *trapped*—within it. Creeping among the tree trunks, lost, wild, graceless and doomed.

But I shook my head and lied to Jane as though I were my brother. I lied to save her, though, to save both of us.

"I do not know what you mean," I told Jane.

Then I left the room.

❦

I ALREADY KNEW JANE HAD been seeing the woman in the wallpaper, because I had continued reading her journals when she escaped the room for walks in the afternoon. The pattern, to her, moved in the night, was still in the daytime, but always the woman imprisoned in the wallpaper's forest would come forward in the moonlight and rattle the bars of her cage. Jane did not want anyone to know what she'd been seeing, so I suspect her questioning of me was in order to discover whether I, too, could see the direction her mind was taking. I suspect she was wondering if I would reveal her to John, as she had remarked in her journal that she sees me quite as a warden.

Oh Jane, I thought. *I want nothing but to free us.*

I did see the direction her mind was taking, but I lied so that Jane would not discover me watching her, as I did throughout the days and nights. How often had I sat beneath her window, waiting for a streamer of moonlight to alight upon her pale face? How often had I watched from the hallway, my feet silent on the floorboards, peering through the sliver of space her open door afforded me at night, with the bed clothing tangled between her legs, and her legs bare and gleaming like ivory?

This was something my brother knew about when he convinced my poor ill father to place my inheritance in his care until I married. John knew about my...*problem*. The problem of my desire. The problem of my desire (*say it!*) for women. John had seen this in me several years ago, when I had turned sixteen and, after church one day, I had taken the hand of my closest friend Margaret Cummings and led her into the woods, where I had kissed her and kissed her and kissed her. My hands cupped her cheeks and she held her lips up to me like a chalice for me to sip from. We had been like this for some time, had kept it our secret. But John had noticed us leaving and he had followed behind, had hid in shadow, watching our secret kissing. When we had finished with our lovemaking, he had stepped away from his hiding place to reveal himself. Margaret gasped, burst into tears immediately, and promptly ran away. Afterward, John had shaken his head at me while grinning. "How shall I explain this to father?" he had asked.

"Please don't," I begged him.

"What would you do to silence me?"

"I will never see her again," I said, thinking that would appease him, thinking he only wanted me to break off such a relation.

But John was not truly concerned with our relationship. No. I should have known that. "We will keep it between us," John said, and when our father had agreed to his suggestion for placing my inheritance into John's hands until I married, I knew the price I had paid for his silence.

I saw the woman in the wallpaper. I saw the creeping women crawling through the gardens too.

But Jane could not know the truth. I could not let her see me. Why, one day, as I stood in her room while she had gone out walking, I had placed my hand upon the yellow wallpaper myself, stroking its patterns and wishing that my life could be other than the one I found myself in, and was startled to hear Jane's voice behind me, suddenly calling my attention.

"What are you doing with the paper, Jennie?" she asked, very quietly, very calmly, and it was as if I had been caught in the forest touching Margaret again.

I turned round quickly, my face hot and red. "Nothing," I said, very short and sharp. "And why have you crept up on me like this? Are you trying to frighten me? Really, Jane."

I moved to go past her, to escape the room, which now felt suffocating, but stopped beside her. "That yellow wallpaper stains everything," I said, angrily. "It has smooched all of your clothes. And John's too," I added. "I wish you both would be more careful!"

I should not have treated Jane in this way, and I knew it even as I brushed past her and closed the door to my own room behind me. I should not have betrayed my feelings. *Any* feelings. Once one is loose, they are like threads, and will continue to unravel until nothing is left of the garment they once comprised. And there I was, pacing the length of my room, back and forth, cursing myself for allowing a loose thread to reveal itself.

Oh, Jane, I thought. *If only you knew how I feel for you. If only you know how much I love you. How better I am than what my brother has made of me. I am his prisoner, as are you. Together, we could free one another.*

And then I quickly debased myself for entertaining such nonsense. John. I could hear him laughing if he'd been able to read my thoughts right then. *Silly Jennie. Silly, silly Jennie.*

It was in those moments of self-denigration, however, that I also decided to find a way to save Jane and myself. I did not know how long it might take before a path would open, but I would wait, I determined right then, until a path in that confusing forest revealed itself.

❧

WHILE JOHN WAS IN TOWN seeing to patients in the days that led up to our leave-taking, Jane took a turn for the worse. She began to peel the layers of the yellow wallpaper off up at the top of the room, little by little, until only parts of it were left, crossing the room like hazy yellow clouds. When John returned, we would return to our own house, but Jane was seized by her obsession and would not leave her room. She declared that she was tearing the wallpaper off out of spite, and I admitted to her that I wouldn't mind doing the same thing, which elicited a laugh from Jane, something I had not heard her do in many months. She smiled at me, and said I was her favorite, and that she knew I would understand what she was doing. But a feverish look burned in her eyes as she spoke, and I said, "Jane, why don't I sleep with you tonight, since John's away. We can stay up late talking. It will be like we are schoolgirls again."

"Oh, Jennie," she said, "I cannot. For if you were to sleep here with me, I would never be able to rest, and that is what John has assigned me to do at all costs."

I nodded. Jane's wits were damaged, clearly, but they were not dull in the least. She had seen right through me.

Perhaps, I thought, she knew what I wanted, and did not want me back.

So I turned and I took up my duties of packing the house, making certain all of our trunks were properly labeled and that everything would arrive home in good order.

There was much to do, so I was kept busy for the rest of that day and night. Mary was no help at all, and Jane of course would not leave her room.

She had stripped the bed of its clothing and once I swore I went past and saw her biting on a corner of it, though when I turned and looked a second time, she was standing at the window with her hands clasped behind her back like a fine maiden observing the fine, late summer weather.

Later that evening, though, when I went up to bring her down to eat, I found the door closed, and when I turned the handle, it would not open.

She had locked it from within.

"Jane?" I called through the door. "Jane, it's time to eat. Do open the door and come downstairs with me."

But no answer came.

So I called for her again, and rattled the knob, trying to jostle it open without any good fortune. "Jane," I said, "really, this is too much. Open the door, please. You're worrying me, Sister."

"Sister!" Jane called from within her sanctuary suddenly. Then I heard her footsteps on the floorboards and saw her shadow creep beneath the sill, touching the tips of my shoes. "Sister," she said, in a whisper this time, now that only the door separated us. "I will not eat with you tonight, Sister," she said. "You are such a dear sister, though, I promise. But I am not coming out. I have things to attend to."

"Jane…" I said.

But her shadow crept back under the door and her footsteps sounded further and further away from me.

❧

IT WAS A LONG NIGHT full of much worry and much fretting at the door. I could hear her in there, taking down more of the strips of yellow wallpaper, laughing a little every now and then. I went outside several times and looked up at her window, and on one occasion saw her silhouette pass by the glass, but only for a moment. *Oh, Jane*, I thought. *We have lost you to that yellow wallpaper at last, haven't we?*

It was John's doing, in my own opinion, though I knew my own opinion meant very little. So I put it away and gave it no further attention, as I had learned to do over the last few years, since father died and John took control of me. He would be home in the early morning, I knew, and would bring us to the boat in his carriage. I would not bother Jane any longer, I decided. Either she would come out on her own, or John would have to find a way to bring her out of there.

Which is what he did when he arrived in the early hours, and found Mary and me waiting in the foyer, Mary bouncing the baby up and down in an attempt to keep him from crying. Jane had not come down at all, though we heard her moving about in the room, and we told John all that had happened while he'd been away. "Weir Mitchell," was all that he said, nearly under his breath, like a curse, and I began to worry for Jane in a different way, because I knew no good would come from John placing her in the "care" of Weir Mitchell. She would only descend even further into whatever madness had taken her this summer.

John rushed up to the nursery and spoke to her through the door. Not harsh, at least not a first, but quite nicely. And when Jane would not open it for him, he began to shake the knob and to pound a little harder on it, until suddenly he was shouting, "An axe! Bring me an axe, Jennie!"

Of course he would turn to violence so quickly. I didn't know how to stave him off of the idea, but did know I needed to convince him to try some other way. Before I needed to intervene, though, Jane finally answered him.

"John, dear!" she said in the gentlest voice. "The key is down by the front steps, under a plantain leaf!"

That silenced John for a few moments.

Then, very quietly, he said, "Open the door, my darling!"

"I can't," said Jane. "The key is down by the front door under a plantain leaf."

"What are you talking about, my darling?" John asked, and Jane continued to respond with the same answer. The key was down by the front door under a plantain leaf. She had thrown it out the window!

John eventually left her door and rushed down the stairs like a wind, brushing past Mary and me, found the key exactly where Jane had described it had fallen, and rushed back up to unlock the door.

"Stay here," I told Mary, and then I followed behind John like a shadow, concerned that he might show violence to Jane as she had caused so much trouble for him.

But when I reached the top of the stairs, John had already opened the door and was staring into the room, his mouth fallen open in shock. "What is the matter?" he cried suddenly. "What are you doing!"

I heard Jane's answer but did not approach to look beyond John's shoulder. "I've got out at last," said Jane, "in spite of you and Jane. And I've pulled off most of the paper, so you can't put me back!"

Oh dear lord in heaven, I thought, and put my hand to my mouth. *She has been possessed by the creature she saw in the wallpaper.*

And then John did something I never thought I would see in my life. He fainted dead to the floor.

And then suddenly I saw Jane creep over his body, as if it were an obstruction.

"Jane," I cried, but she only continued crawling about the room. "Jane, please," I said. But she could not hear me any longer.

By then John was recovering and began to stand up, groggily, putting one hand to his head, as if his mind was feeling great pain. *Good,* I thought. *You deserve this. You have done this to her.* But then he began to shout at Jane and I saw the flicker of his hand go up in the air as though he might bring it down upon her face to shock her back into herself.

"No, John!" I shouted, and he looked over his shoulder. "There are other ways!" I cried.

For once in his life, my brother seemed to hear me and nodded, assenting. "I will get the rope," he said, and then left the room, brushing past me.

The rope, I thought. *What did he mean to do to her?* I did not want to find out. Jane had suffered enough torture already.

As had I.

So as John passed by me to go back down the stairs, I suddenly found myself stepping in line behind him as he opened the gate at the top of the steps that had once upon a time kept the children from wandering out of the nursery and falling. My arms flew out in front of me, as if they had a life of their own, and my hands found a firm place on his back, and before I could realize what, exactly, I was doing, I had given him a great shove, and was then standing at the top of the stairs watching his body tumble and tumble for what seemed like an eternity, and then finally, eventually, he came to thud against the floor at the bottom.

John's head was at an odd angle. His eyes were open, and it seemed as if he were looking up at me in shock. I put my hand to my mouth, gasping, unable to believe what I had just done, but somehow I was still glad for the outcome of my action. And when Mary suddenly came into view beside his body, holding the baby in her arms, she looked up at me with wide eyes and said, "Miss Jennie, what's happened!"

"He fainted!" I cried immediately. "He saw what's become of Jane and fainted on the stairs as he ran from her!"

Then, from the sliver of John's mouth, a noise escaped. "Jennie," he groaned. "Jennie."

"He is alive, Miss!" said Mary beside him, and she began to kneel and to shift the baby to one arm so that she could reach out to John with the other.

"No!" I said from the top of the stairs. "Do not touch him. It's very important not to move him, Mary, or we could do him more harm. Quick, see that the driver goes into town immediately. Have him bring a physician. Hurry!"

There was much crying and confusion after that, but Mary listened to me, and managed to send the driver for help. And while she was carrying out my instructions, I did what I knew I must.

I took a pillow from Jane's bed and made my way down the staircase. One after the other, the steps creaked and groaned beneath my weight. How much I had carried for the last few years. How much I would give to unburden myself of my shackles.

And for Jane, too. And for the baby. God knows what sort of life John would give the child.

At the bottom of the stairs, I stood over John, my dress drifting across his lips. "Jennie," he said, as if that were the only word he had ever learned in his life. "Jennie, Jennie, Jennie."

No longer would he hurt me. No longer would he torture Jane.

"Yes, John," I said. "It is I. It is your silly Jennie." And I put the pillow over his mouth, gently at first, and then pushed harder and harder, until his eyes widened with the fear he enjoyed bringing out in others, and then it was over.

❧

LATER, THE DRIVER RETURNED WITH a doctor as well as a constable, so that they could make their declarations about John's existence and could observe the horrible truth of Jane's madness, as John had witnessed prior to his fall.

They shook their heads and said what a shame, what a terrible shame it all was.

I agreed—yes, very much so—and nodded.

"What will become of her now?" the doctor asked.

And I—I said the only thing that I could.

"She is my sister," I told them. "She is my sister and my good friend. I have my own inheritance, of course, and we will have what John has left behind. I will take care of her and the child."

After they departed, I helped Jane into a carriage—Mary had already been sent ahead in another with the baby—and then we left that house behind us. We left the yellow wallpaper that Jane had torn down to the floor, we left the creeping women who she claimed to see out of every window of the nursery, and we left whoever it was we had become during our stay there for the summer.

As we drove down the winding path to the dock, rocking with the motion of the rutted roads, I brought out Jane's secret papers, passing my fingertips over them. I had saved them for her before John could find them. They were Jane's thoughts, they were Jane's feelings. They were her thread. They were Jane's music, her black paragraphs and the white spaces of silence between them. "This is your story, Sister," I said. "If you play these lines, you might begin to remember yourself."

After which Jane looked at me with the most mysterious of smiles.

"There was a forest in that wallpaper, Jennie," she whispered. "Did you see it?"

I nodded. "I did," I said, patting her hand in mine. "But we are leaving it behind us. A path is opening itself through the forest, Jane. We are free now. We are free to leave everything behind us."

The fact is, I'm all here—head, hands, legs, and all the rest of it, but it happens I'm invisible. It's a confounded nuisance, but I am. That's no reason why I should be poked to pieces by every stupid bumpkin in Iping, is it?

THE INVISIBLE MAN.
H.G. WELLS, 1897

INVISIBLE
MEN

She SAID HE WAS AN "ex-peer-i-ment-al in-vest-i-gat-or, don't you know?" And lucky for me, I don't catch her looking at me much, so I rolled my eyes at myself in the glass I was cleaning, then set it up on its shelf with my eyes rolling in its surface for a long time after.

She always likens herself to our Lord in Heaven, and clutches her hand at her heart like some poor widow, though she just married for a second time not a year ago, and you'd think she'd be happier with Mr. Hall around to help. Especially when *he* came round and took rooms from them. I might be a bit of a dull-headed girl—that's what my mother always told me, Lord keep her—but I ain't so dull I can't see something's wrong with a person when he comes into the Coach and Horses with his head all wrapped up like some bloody mummy, and thick blue goggles for glasses. Really, I should wince and say to her, "Do you think that's normal, miss?"

Oh, shut up, you silly girl. Move it along. You're slower than a cow! Help indeed! Snap, snap! Clap, clap! She's got many ways of dealing with me. But

I ain't no girl, and I ain't no cow. I got sixteen years, and four of them I been working like anyone. What she sees ain't me, but some other girl. Cause ain't I the one who cleared the straw he spilled from those crates of his all over the floor of his room? And ain't I the one who scrubbed at a stain on the floor he'd made with all his chemicals and such?

She wanted to take him his tea and his eggs and ham. *She* wanted to stand at his shut door and listen to his moaning and sobbing, hand clutched at her heart like some mother. *She* wanted to try speaking with him like she was on his level—whatever it was, it was surely above hers by the way he spoke—and all I could do was laugh behind my hand in the kitchen when he chased her out of that room with a chair, the chair floating in midair like a ghost, and she came shrieking down the staircase.

Mrs. Hall gave me a hot time of it, she did, taking out her troubles with him on the likes of me while he was staying here. But I didn't let her muck me about too much. And there was always talk to be had when she wasn't round the bar, but upstairs leaning her ear against that door of his. Teddy Henfrey was here one day after all that mess with the Invisible Man started, and I caught him looking up at the pub's ceiling, shaking his head. "Here, Millie," he said, "what's Mrs. Hall on to up there? Still trying to get old goggle-eyes to talk?"

I kept wiping glasses and shook my head. "I don't right know, Teddy," I said. "I keep to my own or she'll give me a hot time of it."

And Teddy said, "Ain't like you're to blame for anything, Millie. And anyway, you're mostly back in the kitchen where nobody can see you."

"True enough," I told Teddy. "But when *she* wants to, she can see me all right. When she wants to."

Teddy Henfrey is the village clock-mender. He had a bad round of it with old goggle-eyes on the very day he showed up at the Coach and Horses. Mrs. Hall asked Teddy to come mend a clock in her new guest's room, but that clock had been dead some three months and she'd never once made a glance in its direction. Then goggle-eyes come through the door of the inn on the last day of February, snow blowing all round him, and him wrapped up in a greatcoat, muffler, and a hat with a brim so wide it cast a shadow over his face. And wouldn't you know, not two hours after she brought him his eggs and ham, Mrs. Hall was going on about that clock in his room needing mending.

It was just so she could get in there while Teddy went to work. Anyone could see that. Wanting a look at things, she was. We didn't know goggle-eyes weren't visible when he showed up, of course—we thought he'd been hurt in a fire or some other kind of accident—but if we'd known the truth of him then, I would've liked to say to her, "He's invisible, miss. He ain't blind, too, is he?"

But I must remind myself I've got a place, and that ain't so bad, considering I got no people. Ma died four years ago, and that's when I come to the Coach and Horses, where she'd done the work before me. Dad's been gone since I was little. Drowned, Ma told me, in the river one black night when he was wandering round like a fish with two legs. So I suppose it could have been me coming through that door on the last day of February, shouting, "In the name of human charity! A room and a fire!"

It was the Invisible Man, though. And what happened after that, none of us would've guessed.

What happened was this. Mrs. Hall wouldn't leave the man well enough alone. She kept trying to get his story out of him. Whenever she got a chance, she'd make a reason to barge in, even though he'd said to leave him be. She took him ham and eggs, like I've said, and then, after he waited for her to leave, she came back to the kitchen and saw she'd forgotten the mustard I'd made. "I declare!" she shouted. "Slow as treacle, you are, Millie! Help indeed!" She took the mustard upstairs then, and I pulled a face at her backside, but when she come down again a few minutes later, her face was all wrinkled with trouble.

"What is it, miss?" I asked, truly worried at that point. It's not often Mrs. Hall looks like someone run her over with a carriage.

She stood there for a while, blank, and then finally she started speaking. Said that his injuries must have something to do with his mouth, cause when she pushed in with the mustard, he put his serviette up to his face and wouldn't move it for nothing till she turned to leave.

"Something terrible must have happened to him," I said, and she nodded, staring off into a distance.

You'd have thought that would have been enough to keep a person from going on and bothering with him any more, but not Mrs. Hall. In fact, it wasn't a half hour passed before she took herself back up there, and this time it was to try and make a friend of him.

I suppose I made my own reasons for being round where she was, too. Cause it was something to watch her get to work on him, it was. She was smooth as a confidence man if ever I saw one. Stood there in his room and started telling him about her sister's boy, Tom, who'd cut his arm on a scythe last summer, and how Tom was three months getting better. "My sister was tied up with her little ones, though," she told him, "and there were all those bandages of Tom's to do and undo every day. So I took to changing the bandages as a way of helping, and by the end of that summer I knew my way round wrapping and unwrapping people." She paused after she finished her story, to make her point, and what she told the Invisible Man at the end of her ramble was, "If I may make so bold as to say it, sir—"

Before she could finish making so bold, though, old goggle-eyes interrupted to say, "Will you get me some matches? My pipe is out."

I had to put my hand over my mouth when I heard that one out in the hall where I'd been putting away the bedding. He pulled her right up, he did. But she got him those matches he asked for, and she never did make so bold as to say anything else.

Later that day was when she brought in Teddy Henfrey, like I mentioned, to make a show of fixing that dead clock. But Teddy stayed over his welcome. Kept trying to fix things about that clock that didn't need fixing, just so he could get a look at our strange houseguest. So it weren't just Mrs. Hall who was curious. I suppose anyone with a mind that notices things wanted a look at him. But when it was clear Teddy was wasting his time on that clock, goggle-eyes told him that's exactly what he was doing, and sent him right off. I hear Teddy went round town in a tizzy about how a man must do a clock at times, surely!

That was probably the first mistake, if you want to start counting the important ones, the ones that started other things happening. Mrs. Hall let Teddy in the man's room for her own reasons, and when the Invisible Man threw Teddy out, Teddy went about town like a cloud spewing thunder and lightning. It was Teddy, you see, who ran across Mr. Hall coming back from his conveyance route to Sidderbridge Junction and told him, "You got a rum-looking customer at the Coach and Horses, Hall!"

And when Mr. Hall said he didn't know what Teddy was on about, Teddy told him how Mrs. Hall let a room to a stranger, and how she didn't even know the bloke's name, and how he was all done up with bandages over his face, and how tufts of black hair curled out of the man's wrappings like the horns of the devil.

He planted a seed in Mr. Hall right then, and when Mr. Hall come round the Coach and Horses a bit later, all totted up with whisky, he started giving Mrs. Hall a time of it. And when Mrs. Hall just kept on as if he weren't even there, he started saying things like, "You women don't know everything!" and that's when Mrs. Hall turns round real slow, to give him a dark eye, and says, "You mind your own business, Hall, and I'll mind mine!"

I dare say I had a laugh about that one. Caught it in my hand, though, and slipped it in my pocket. She was always giving me a hot time of it, she was, but she'd take her tongue out and do Mr. Hall a bad turn whenever the feeling came on her. Couldn't help but feel a bit bad for him, but also a bit like I weren't the only one she didn't see till she wanted to.

❧

IT WAS THE NEXT DAY, though, that things really started to seem strange, if that's possible. His luggage was brought over from the rail station, and it was all in large crates. Mr. Fearenside and Mr. Hall started to unload them from the cart outside the inn, and you could see how heavy the crates were by the strain in their faces, how red their cheeks turned, like roses in winter.

The Invisible Man came through the pub where I was collecting plates for a table, and brushed right past me like a cold wind. He was wearing his greatcoat and was muffled in that hat and gloves and scarf, just like the day before. I went to the window and rubbed away the fog of my breath to watch him go clattering down the steps, shouting that Mr. Fearenside and Mr. Hall were taking too long, and why weren't his things already unloaded. It were a bad idea for him to go down so quick and angry like that, though, cause Mr. Fearenside's dog was under the wagon, see, and out it come, barking and yapping, and took a nip at the Invisible Man's hand. Old goggle-eyes pulled back his leg and gave the dog a good kick, but that just stirred the thing even more, and the next thing it did was lunge at his leg and take away a piece of his trousers.

Then—*snap! snap!*—Mr. Fearenside give his dog two licks of a whip, and the dog went yelping back under the wagon.

Goggle-eyes come through the pub door directly, cursing under his breath. I take a glance at the place where the dog tore his trousers, expecting to see a leg in there, and thinking I might get a chance of seeing what ails his skin as to require all those wrappings. But there ain't any leg I can see as that bit of his trouser opens and shuts like the flap of a carnival tent, giving glimpses of darkness behind it.

Seemed nothing was in there at all. Just darkness. And I thought, *How can that be? Man needs a leg to keep walking.*

He slammed his door when he reached his bedroom, and after a few minutes, Mr. Hall come in to see if the guest got hurt in a bad way. But Mr. Hall made the mistake—the second big mistake—of going in without knocking.

There was a tussle of some sort up there. Anyone with ears in the house could hear it. First Mr. Hall made an awful sound, then the door slammed shut again. A minute later, Mr. Hall's back in the pub, rubbing his head like someone's given him a great clout upside it.

"Are you all right, sir?" I asked, and he looked up, noticing me as if it's the first he's ever seen me. He didn't say anything, though. Just tugged at his mustache and winced, shook his head like a dog wringing itself out, then went back out to help with the unloading.

The crates were brought in then, one after another, once goggle-eyes came out of his room wearing a new pair of trousers. And what a spectacle, the things those crates carried! Towers of books. Glass tubes, glass bottles. And all kinds of powders and fluids of all sorts of colors. A burner and a balance. The Invisible Man put his things wherever he could find a bit of room. On the mantel. On the bookshelf. On the windowsill. On the floor, when he had no more room to speak of. Quite a sight it all was, too. Took the breath right from me when I peeked round the door to see inside. It appeared he was about to open a chemist's shop right there in the Coach and Horses!

He got right to work, too, for the rest of the day, with the door locked so Mr. and Mrs. Hall couldn't come in whenever they wanted. Sometimes I'd take a journey up the stairs to get a dustbin or a set of bedding for another room, and would take my time to listen near his door. Bottles clinked. Fluids dripped. I could hear a pencil scratch across paper, and thought of him then, bent over one of those big books, all taken up by some idea or experiment that possessed him. And while I was lost in thought of him like that was when *she* came round the corner and gasped like I were burgling.

"Millie!" she said, and I jumped back from his door, embarrassed at first, and then angry with her. Ain't it her, after all, who'd been doing the same thing I'd been doing right then, and even more?

The door opened on us then, and goggle-eyes looked back and forth between us. I shivered, being that close to him, seeing him look down at me through those blue spectacles of his. And his nose—what a shiny thing it was to see this close. Like a toy nose he might have purchased at a shop somewhere, it was. Mrs. Hall took the chance to look past him into the room right then, and before goggle-eyes could give us a bad time, she gasps and says, "My word, but it looks like a barn in here! All that straw, sir!"

"Put it on my bill, if you must," goggle-eyes muttered.

Mrs. Hall didn't stop there, though. No, she was in motion. Pushed right past him into the room and found her way to a golden stain he'd made on the floor with some of his chemicals, just like a hound, and said, "Sir, my floor!"

And goggle-eyes just said, "The bill, put it on the bill, I told you!"

I took the chance to slip away while they haggled over the price of his damages. Later, though, Mrs. Hall said to go in and sweep things up, the straw and all, and try to get that golden stain out.

I did as told, but I never did tell anyone what happened later that day when I went up there. Not even that writer, Mr. Wells, when he came round months after, looking to collect the scraps of the story from us.

❧

THIS IS WHAT HAPPENED THAT day, the day I've never told a soul about.

I show up at his door and knock gently, as Mrs. Hall said to, and when he doesn't come to the door, I call through it, "Millie, sir. Here to sweep up, if you'll let me."

But still no answer comes. I look over my shoulder, back down the stairwell. I can hear Mrs. Hall down in the kitchen making tea. Then I look back at his door, turn the knob, and odd but it ain't locked as usual. And when I push in, the room's empty. Not the straw or mess, of course. Him. Old goggle-eyes ain't there. But I've not seen him come down and I've been working in the parlour all morning. And I've not seen him go out the pub way either, and I been working in there all afternoon. And as Mrs. Hall made it a thing for me to knock, like she expects him to be in there working on his experiments, I can't imagine she seen him leave the Coach and Horses either.

So I go in and think, Maybe this is better, not having to see him. Just doing my business of picking up after, and getting away without having to work around him. There are lots of things out of order in there, so I start first with the straw, since it's most noticeable, and sweep it all up into a pile in the hall to pick up later. Then I start in on the stain, putting my elbow and shoulder into it. It ain't coming out well, though I do manage to make it fade a little. I rub and rub and finally I sigh, sit up on my knees, and stretch my arms above me, letting my fingers flicker in the air, stretching them too.

And that's when I feel it. Something creeping under my arms, like spiders crawling on my skin. I put my arms down quick and the feeling goes away. I look both right and left, but no one's in there. Just me. I bend over again, thinking I've got to get a day free if Mrs. Hall will allow it. I'll tell her the spiders-on-my-arms story, I'm thinking, and that might help my case. And while I'm rubbing at that golden stain on the floor, thinking about this, I feel the spiders go crawling down my spine.

I sit up again and say, "Who's there?"

That's when the spiders come walking over my right cheek, and I shiver. I open my mouth, ready to scream, and that's when his hand goes over my mouth, catching my scream fore I can get it out of me.

"Shh, shh, girl," he says. "Shh, shh." Like I'm a baby crying. So I stop making a fuss and he says, "I will release you if you promise to be quiet." I nod once, and then his hand comes off my mouth.

"Who?" I say. And then, "What are you?"

He says, "Who I am is not important, Millie. What I am is invisible."

"Are you a ghost?" I say, looking round the room at nothing. I hear footsteps on the floor, creaking in a room where no one's walking. I stand, ready to run.

"Ah," he says, chuckling. "A village girl, through and through. No, my young one, I am no ghost. I am a scientist, you see."

And I say, "I don't see nothing."

He laughs at that. The room laughs at that. I say, "What's so funny about the truth?"

He says, "The truth? The truth is humorous more often than not, if you have the right perspective."

I don't say anything to that. I'm too busy looking round the room, trying to hear where the footsteps come from. He's circling me like wolves circle lambs cut off from the herd.

Then the footsteps stop, and he says, "I have discovered something, Millie. A powerful thing. The secret of invisibility. A way for no one to ever see you."

I say, "Not many people care to see me as it is. What's so powerful about that?"

"Well, exactly," he says, and his voice changes so it sounds like he's latched on to something. "Exactly, Millie. You're already an unseen, of sorts, aren't you? And what good does it do you? If you were truly invisible, though, you could do what you can't now. You could take a greater payment for the work you do. You could damage those who regularly abuse your services."

I wince, thinking I'm not understanding what I'm hearing. "Sir," I say. "Are you talking about thieving?"

"I'm talking about taking what you deserve," he tells me. "Taking what you deserve and much, much more." He says, "Millie, I can offer you a moment in history, if you should like to join me."

"History?" I say, blinking. "What good is a moment in history, sir?"

"You will never die, Millie. Your name will live on forever if you join my ranks of the invisible. You will be remembered."

His fingers—I know that's what they are this time round—caress my cheek again, a soft stroke. I notice that old goggle-eyes has his greatcoat hanging up in the corner now, and his hat on the table, and his gloves beside it. His trousers hang over the back of a chair. His shoes sit beside the legs of his chemistry table. "It's you," I say, "ain't it? You ain't wearing any clothes, are you?"

He don't answer me none, and I hear his steps move away from me. Then, from the table with all his tubes and bottles set up on it, a needle filled with blue fluid lifts into the air like a bottle fly, and starts drifting toward me.

"Would you like to test my new serum, Millie?" he says. "Would you like to be powerful like I am?"

I back up without saying anything. The needle follows. At the door, I take hold of the knob and say, "Sir, nothing's happened here today.

I want you to understand that. You can go about your business and I'll go about mine. Not a word they'll have from me, but I promise they'll have it if you don't leave me be."

I close the door without a word back from him. I turn to find the mound of straw in the hall behind me. I lean over then, pick up as much as I can carry, and take it downstairs. Mrs. Hall don't see me take it out the kitchen door. She's busy doing sums of some sort on the account book. Totting up what goggle-eyes owes her, surely.

❧

THE REST OF THAT DAY was taken up by thinking about what happened, and after a while my thoughts just kept spinning out like a spider web, and at some point in the spinning, I started thinking on my mother.

I hadn't thought about her for a while. It'd been four years since she died. I was twelve then, and working at the Coach and Horses kept me busy enough over the following years that I didn't think much about anything but my duties. I can't say when for sure I'd stopped fingering my memories of Ma, but surely it was sometime between washing the dishes and making up beds.

My mother had been a good woman, even if she were sometimes hard on me. Like I said, she sometimes called me dull-headed, and would come home from the Coach and Horses and shoo me off cause she'd been caring after others all day, and there I was wanting a bit of her when she didn't have a drop left. Usually, though, after she got her feet up and her wind back, she'd sit me on her lap and brush my hair. She'd tell me stories. In all her stories, I was the heroine. Millie who went to London on the back of a flying horse. Millie who found a cave where the fair folk live, and brought them home to help her poor mother cook and clean. Cause of Ma, I had many ideas of myself that I can't say I'd thought of on my own. But they were none of them the *me* I was after she died, after I went to take her place at the Coach and Horses.

I wonder sometimes, what sort of idea of herself did Ma have? She never put herself in her stories as a heroine, just me. And whenever I tried to include her, she'd say, "Aww, Millie, my love, your old mother's not an adventurer like you are."

Quite an adventure it was, too, after she died. Going to live with the Halls, working there like my mother did. And then the funeral service, when some of her friends from the village came to pay their respects, that was shorter than I'd expected. I suppose I'd imagined something grander, rows of flowers, a violin playing somewhere, at least a piano, or a choir— even one melancholy singer, really—might have marked my mother's passing. But, no, that was not to be. At least the vicar Mr. Bunting was nice about her, from what I remember. He mentioned the smile she had for anyone who entered the Coach and Horses. I remember thinking how odd that was, though, cause she weren't ever smiling when she came home from there.

She has a stone marker in the churchyard now, but her name ain't on it. Sometimes, when I have a free day, I sit with her there, and trace my fingertip over the dirt on the stone. I spell her name. Rose. I trace the letters over and over, until it burns the tip of my finger.

That's what I kept coming back to after that incident in the Invisible Man's room. How he said I could have a moment in history. My mother never had a moment in history. Her name ain't even on that stone in the churchyard. All that's left of her is that stone itself, and whatever I can recall of her.

❧

WHAT WOULD MA HAVE THOUGHT of the Invisible Man, I wonder? Would she have had a smile for him, like the vicar Mr. Bunting said she had for anyone? I certainly didn't give goggle-eyes any smiles for the rest of the time he stayed at the Coach and Horses. Which was a long time, indeed. He came in on the last day of February and stayed all through March and April. Everyone in the village had something to say about him, too, they did. Even the people who'd never chanced to see him. Children made up songs and rhymes. They called him the Bogey Man, and sometimes you'd see a whole pack of them running down a lane, and someone would pull them up and ask where they were all going in a hurry, and they'd say, "John seen the Bogey Man walking this way! We're going to see him!" And then they'd be off again, singing their Bogey Man songs.

Teddy Henfrey stopped coming to the Coach and Horses after a while. Said it made him feel too uncomfortable, being there, hearing old goggle-eyes thrashing about in his room, doing his experiments. Mr. Hall complained he was driving business away. But I thought it was really Teddy Henfrey doing the driving, cause he was the one going round the village telling people how he won't go back to the Coach and Horses for a pint until that Bogey Man is gone. Mrs. Hall told Mr. Hall, "Bills settled punctual is bills settled punctual, whatever you'd like to say about it." She said maybe she'd made a mistake, marrying a man who didn't know the ways of an inn like her father had, and that they'd wait till summer to do anything about it. Mr. Hall went off muttering something fierce, and for the rest of that day everyone stayed away from him.

I can't say goggle-eyes went out much in the two months he come to stay here. Mostly he worked in the parlour he'd set up as a chemist's shop, and spent his nights walking his bedroom floor. Even though Mrs. Hall spent time listening at his door, she couldn't make heads or tails of anything she heard in there, but I never stopped to have a listen any longer. When it was time for sleep, I swept past his door fast as a mouse, and ran up the stairs to the attic, hoping he didn't hear me.

But everyone knew he was up in that room of his in the Coach and Horses, even if they didn't see him but now and then, when he took walks round the village for fresh air, usually at twilight or late in the evenings. And so talk began to spread, wondering about what sort of work he did, or if he were a criminal all bandaged up like that to hide himself from the authorities. And when this kind of talk began to make its way back to the Coach and Horses, Mrs. Hall come right out to the center of the pub one night when we had a decent crowd, and called everyone's attention to her.

"I've heard all your nonsense talk," she said in a firm voice, "and I'll say this once and once only. He is an ex-peer-i-ment-al in-vest-i-ga-tor, is what he is! Now stop your tale telling."

"A scientist," Mr. Hall muttered from behind the bar. And when Mrs. Hall shot him a look, he went back to pouring.

"Yes, quite right," said Mrs. Hall, turning back to her audience. "A scientist." She seemed to think the folks at the pub would hear all that as an explanation, and go back to their business. Which I thought odd, since Mrs. Hall's been living in Iping all her life, and surely she must know that everyone talking about anything different going on in the village is their exact business.

"Here, Millie!" Mr. Fearenside said that same night, after most everyone had left and I was cleaning up the tables. "What do you make of old goggle-eyes? You have to live right here with him, after all. What's your story?"

I looked up from the table I'd been wiping down and met Mr. Fearenside's eyes for a moment, then looked toward the staircase that led up to the Invisible Man's room. He could be standing there, on that bottom step, for all I knew. He could be watching me, waiting to see me break my word with him. I'd felt his eyes on me many a time over March and April, and I was worse than a cat all that time, jumping at no cause a time or two every day it might seem to anyone looking. I could feel him watching me, waiting for me to tell his secret. So when I turned back to Mr. Fearenside, I said, "I ain't got no story, Mr. Fearenside. I don't see nothing and nothing don't see me. Simple as that."

"Clever girl, Millie!" said Mr. Fearenside.

And Mrs. Hall appeared in the pub right then to say, "Brought her up right, I can see now."

I didn't say anything to that. Just went back to wiping and taking up glasses. But for the rest of the night I kept thinking, *How?* How could she say that? *She* didn't bring me up. It were my mother's hands that molded me.

And right then, as I thought that, I started to cry a little. Tried getting the tears out of my eyes fore anyone saw them, but it was no use. Mrs. Hall saw straightaway and said, "Now what, Millie? I swear, always crying about something, you are!"

❧

WHAT HAPPENED NEXT, EVERYONE KNOWS by now. It's been months gone by since they found and killed him over in Port Burdock, and even now there's always something about the other invisible folks he made that keep going round the countryside, terrifying innocent people and stealing. What happened was, Mr. Cuss, the village doctor, turned up at the Coach and Horses at the end of April. Had a professional interest in our guest, he said, since old goggle-eyes were all wrapped up in bandages. Said others were worried he was sick with something that might go round. But Mrs. Hall told Mr. Cuss he don't have a reason to see her guest if her guest ain't asked to be seen. Mr. Cuss went right on by her, though, into goggle-eyes' room, where they must have had some kind of conversation, because he didn't come out again for at least ten minutes.

Whatever they talked about ended in a short cry of surprise from Mr. Cuss, and then we heard a chair flung to the side, and that sharp bark of a laugh that belonged to goggle-eyes. Then the quick patter of feet to the door where Mrs. Hall and I both stood listening with our ears turned. It opened, and there stood Mr. Cuss. His face was pale as whitewash, and he held his hat against his chest like he were going to give us bad news. He looked back and forth at us, but in the end he said nothing, not a whisper, just went past us and down the stairs as if the devil himself were on his heels, and then the pub door closed behind him.

The Invisible Man laughed softly in the room beyond, and Mrs. Hall, without peering in, asked if she could get him anything. "No," he said. His voice sounded black as the blacking I'd put on the stove that morning. "There is nothing anyone can get me now, Mrs. Hall. It is over."

Mrs. Hall stood there for a minute, twisting her hands in her apron, waiting to see if he might say more. Maybe she hoped he'd ask for something and make her useful, I can't right say. But when she turned and saw me, she jumped back an inch, as if she'd forgotten I'd been at the door with her all that time. "Millie," she said. "Kitchen." Then she went down the hall to her own room, shut the door, and didn't come out until the next day, when we heard that the vicar Mr. Bunting and his wife had been burgled. And on Whit Monday, no less.

❧

THE STORY MADE IT ROUND town like the plague everyone feared old
goggle-eyes might carry underneath those bandages of his. Before noon
everyone knew the vicar and his wife had woken in the small hours of the
morning by the sound of coins rattling downstairs. And when they went
to check on the noise, found a candle lit. And the door unbolted. But no
one there. They swore they watched the door of their house open and
close on its own like it had a spirit in it. And then, when they checked their
cash drawer, it was empty.

That same afternoon, while I was making a soup in the kitchen, a
great racket happened up in old goggle-eyes' room. I heard Mrs. Hall
screaming like her head must have come right off and started flying round
the rooms on its own, and then it come down the steps and found me like
that, making soup in the kitchen. I looked up, dropped my knife, and went
up directly.

I found Mr. Hall holding her up in the hallway. Old goggle-eyes' door
was closed up behind them. She slouched in Mr. Hall's arms like she might
faint at any time, so I got my arm under her other side and together Mr. Hall
and I brought her down to the pub and I poured her a cup of rum to calm
her. She and Mr. Hall took turns then, telling me what had happened.

Seems they went up because old goggle-eyes' door was open, but
he weren't in there, and his clothes were all laid out, and his bed cold,
which meant he'd been gone all morning, but without clothes, and all
of his bandages left behind too. Mrs. Hall said he'd put spirits into her
furniture, cause didn't her mother's own chair lift up and chase her right
out of the room? I didn't stop her to say it weren't any spirits in that chair,
but old goggle-eyes himself lifting it and chasing her out the door with it.
How could I? If the Halls knew I'd known our guest had been invisible
all this time and didn't tell, I'm not sure what would happen. They might
take me out the door directly, and leave me to find my own way. So I kept
my mouth shut and kept nodding as Mrs. Hall brought the story round to
when I'd come up the stairs after hearing her screaming.

"Out," she told Mr. Hall now, after she'd finished the story. "Lock the doors on him! I don't want him here any longer! All of those bottles and powders! I knew there wasn't something right with him. No one should have that many bottles!"

I held her hand while she sipped her drink, and didn't say what came to my mind right then. Ain't it her who defended him some weeks ago? Ain't it her who said he was an *ex-peer-i-men-tal in-vest-i-ga-tor*, like that were something above the rest of us? I figure she'd had a bad enough time already. When she finished her rum, I poured another to help her get along a little further.

She asked me to go across the way to get Mr. Wadgers, the blacksmith, to come and have a look at that furniture. She admired Mr. Wadgers, she said. She said she wanted his opinion on the strange occurrences at the Coach and Horses. So I ran over and brought Mr. Wadgers back, telling him very little, as I didn't want to put an idea into his mind before he had a chance to think for himself.

"Thank you, Millie," said Mrs. Hall when we returned. She sighed and began telling Mr. Wadgers about our morning, and I thought the madness had surely passed, that old goggle-eyes had had a good time of giving her a fright, and now he'd go back to his experiments. But soon as Mrs. Hall's sigh escaped her lips, wouldn't you know, the door upstairs creaks open, and down the stairs he comes, dressed in his bandages and hat and coat and muffler, just like when he first appeared in the late February entrance to the Coach and Horses. "I didn't see him come in," said Mrs. Hall as he walked past, as though none of us were there for the seeing, and went to his chemistry parlour, where he shut the door.

Mr. Hall got up and followed after Mr. Wadgers told him he should do so. He knocked at the door, opened it a sliver, and demanded an explanation for old goggle-eyes' sudden appearance. But the only thing old goggle-eyes had to say was, "Go to the devil! And shut that door behind you!"

And for the rest of that morning all we could hear was him in there clinking his bottles and tubes together, tossing about all those chemicals.

❦

IT WAS LATER, AFTER WE'D all gone back to our regular ways, that Mrs. Hall brought the thing to an end. It was her, I'd say, that had the courage to do so. She gave me instructions not to feed old goggle-eyes a crumb, and to not heed his calls. Instead, we went about our business, and ignored him as he threw bottles into his fireplace and cursed the gods. I cringed whenever I heard him shouting in there, but Mrs. Hall said, "Be a rock, Millie," and so I was still as the stone that marks my mother's grave in the churchyard.

At midday, though, he opened his door and demanded Mrs. Hall attend to him. His shouts filled up the Coach and Horses. Mrs. Hall hitched up her skirts and went right to him, her fright from the morning having passed her by, and said, "Is it your bill you're wanting, sir?"

"Why have I not received my breakfast?" he asked.

And Mrs. Hall said, "Why isn't my bill paid? That's what I'd like to know."

I put my hand over my mouth, knowing that I could shut myself up and hold my voice inside me, even if Mrs. Hall had no way of doing so for her own sake.

He told her he had the money he owed, but Mrs. Hall wasn't backing down. She said, "Yes, but I wonder where you found it. The vicar and his wife been burgled this very morning, and yesterday you had none." Then she began demanding he tell her what he'd done to her chairs—had he put spirits in them? And she demanded to know what he was on to in there with all those bottles and fluids. She demanded to know how his room was empty that morning and how he got in and out with none of us seeing. She demanded to know his name. "Who are you?" she said.

An endless list of demands, it was, and when Mrs. Hall reached the end of it, old goggle-eyes stamped his foot like the hoof of the devil and said, "By Heaven! I will show you!"

Mind you, I was in the kitchen when all this was happening. I could hear Mrs. Hall's voice going up and up, though, and stopped washing the dishes for a moment to listen harder. And just as I took my hands out of the water, Mrs. Hall screamed. And the scream was something louder and more frightening than anything she'd made when the chair flew at her earlier that morning.

I had my hands in my apron, drying them off, when I come out the kitchen into the pub, and there, right in front of me, his back to me, was old goggle-eyes. But he'd taken the bandages off his head, and his goggles and hat. He was a headless man standing there, and even though I'd already been in a room with him when he was invisible, I couldn't help but catch Mrs. Hall's screams and join her in sending one up to our Lord in Heaven.

It was a bad thing to do, though, it was. For it only called his attention. Old goggle-eyes turned round when he heard me, and though I couldn't see his face, I knew he was going to kill me. He'd blame me, I knew, for his discovery. Even if it were Mrs. Hall who'd forced him to reveal himself. To reveal that there weren't a self underneath all those bandages.

I turned and ran back into the kitchen then, and he came after, calling, "Millie, Millie!" But I kept on going. I took the stairs up to the next floor, and then the stairs up to my room in the attic. I locked the door, then opened my window, flung my head out and saw people running not only out of the pub beneath me, squealing and screaming, but also up and down the street people were abandoning the Whit Monday festivities to see what was happening down at the Coach and Horses.

Gypsies and sweets sellers, the swing man, wenches and dandies— they all came running down to the inn, and soon I could hear their voices burbling up from below like the soup I'd left on the stove. It was like how the vicar Mr. Bunting talked to us one Sunday about the tower of Babel, and all the many voices, and how no sense could be made of anything. I didn't move from my seat on the ledge of my dormer window, only looked over my shoulder every now and then to see if my door were still closed. I had the key in the palm of my hand, sweaty and hot. And later, when Mrs. Hall come up to say through the door that all was fine again, that the Invisible Man were gone now, they'd chased him off after a struggle, and won't you come out Millie, I opened that hand and saw how I'd held the key so tight it had cut into my skin and raised my blood.

❧

WHAT DID HE WANT FROM me, I wonder sometimes, when he ran after me into the kitchen, calling my name out? I was afraid then, and didn't stop to ask. But when I look back now, I sometimes think I can see round that fear to hear his voice again. To understand that he weren't angry at me, like I thought. He'd sounded frightened as I was. The same way I sometimes come into a room and see a mouse, and both of us jump at the sight of each other. What did he want from me? Someone told me that, after I ran away, the constable came and found him sitting at the kitchen table eating a crust of bread and some cheese. Was that all he'd wanted? Really? Had he just been hungry?

I can't right know the answer to that question. After that day, he only came back to Iping once more, with a tramp he forced to help him steal his books out of the room where he stayed here at the Coach and Horses. When he had those books again, they say he went on to other places and grew madder and madder, and stole more and more, and even involved himself in murder before a mob in Port Burdock hunted him down and killed him. It took a few weeks before the various stories told by various people in the various nearby ports and villages he terrorized were brought out and put together, so that a bigger story could be seen. And that was mostly cause of the writer, Mr. Wells, who came round after everything seemed to be over, drawing us all out to speak with him. Everyone, that is, except me.

He was a curious man, Mr. Wells, with eyes that pierced through me in a way that made me feel too seen. So much so that, when it was my turn for an interview, I said, "I don't have anything I can tell you, sir. I'm sorry."

"And why is that, Millie?" he asked as I sat at a table in the pub with him, rubbing my fingertips over the palm of my hand where the key had cut into me. "I hear, after all, that you were here almost all the time, and that he chased you into the kitchen on the day he revealed himself."

"I don't see nothing, sir," I told him. "And nothing sees me."

Mr. Wells waited for me to look up from my fidgeting before he spoke again. And when I did, he said, "I don't believe that for an instant, Millie."

But he let me alone, he did, and I was grateful.

❧

IT WAS CLEAR THAT THE Invisible Man had given the same offer he'd made me to others. Mrs. Hall read the news to me every morning in the months that followed his reign of terror. One day she said, "Look here, Millie! Not two months after he's been killed in Port Burdock and there are others like him taking on his filthy business. Thieving and firing houses! What a world we live in! If I had it my way, I'd see them all out of the country!"

"Would you now, miss?" I said. "And how would you see to it, them being invisible and all?"

She gave me a sour face and said, "Millie, you know what I mean."

I met her eyes when she said that, instead of looking down at the floor like I used to when she scolded. I never say what I think aloud, of course, but there are words that eyes can say just as well as any mouth can. And what my eyes said that morning when they met hers was, "You was wrong about him all along, weren't you?" An experimental investigator, indeed.

I think about the description of his death Mrs. Hall read from Mr. Wells' report some months later, usually when I'm alone and can use my time to imagine what happened after he was finished with us here at the Coach and Horses. She said that the people of Port Burdock welcomed him with fists and knees and boots when they finally cornered him. She said that they welcomed him with the flash of their teeth and a spade to the head, swung heavily. She said that, when he no longer moved and they began to back away, he started to appear within the circle they'd made round him.

First, an old woman saw a hand. Just the nerves and veins and arteries and bones could be seen beneath the invisible flesh. But then there were his feet as well. And then, slowly, his skin began to appear, moving inward from his toes and fingers toward the center of his body, like waves returning to the sea. He was all bashed up and bloody. His skin was white, his eyes red like a rabbit's. Nearly an albino, he'd been.

Mrs. Hall says he'd been a working boy who grew up and went to university somehow. Said his teachers ignored him. Said he stole from his own father to pay for his experiments, and that his father killed himself when he found the money gone, for he needed it to pay a debt.

I shake my head and say, "It's a bad business, it is."

And Mrs. Hall says, "I don't know who these scientists think they are. Playing as if they were our Lord in Heaven."

I don't say, "I meant his teachers ignoring him, miss."

Mrs. Hall says, "They'll get these other ones, too. You wait and see."

I say, "Indeed, miss."

❦

SUNDAYS, WHEN I GO ROUND to Ma's grave after church, I think on the scene when they killed him, and wonder if the other people he injected with the serum he offered me were there when it happened, watching, invisible, protected if they did not speak and make themselves known. Did his anger at the world that didn't see him get into them as well? Surely it must have, as they've continued his terrible ways after his passing. That is what he leaves behind. Now, no one will forget him.

And then I wonder about his offer. A moment in history. Sometimes, when I'm looking at my mother's stone, tracing the letters of her name into the dirt that covers it, I wonder if I should have taken him up on it. For what good is life without the howls of anger in a world that thinks so highly of itself, even when there is great wrongness in it?

To be seen, to be known. It seems, when I look out at the faces of the people in the village, that's what most want. But we live in a world where not everyone can possibly be seen. We put too much on seeing to know one another, and the eye is a friend who often lies. At least this is something I've noticed in my time pouring drinks and making beds at the Coach and Horses. It might be better, I sometimes think, if we were all blind.

Proof of my time here. That is my desire. But there's little most can do to have this. The choices for our memorials are few, like Ma's unmarked stone here. I trace her name again, and again. We must take what we are given, then, like the vicar Mr. Bunting is always reminding us, and be happy. We must be happy, I think, with our anger, with our outraged mobs, with our eagerness to tear at the world that binds us. We must be content with what we have.

When Aunt Em came there to live she was
a young, pretty wife. The sun and wind had
changed her, too. They had taken the sparkle
from her eyes and left them a sober gray; they had
taken the red from her cheeks and lips, and they were gray
also. She was thin and gaunt, and never smiled now. When
Dorothy, who was an orphan, first came to her, Aunt Em had
been so startled by the child's laughter that she would scream
and press her hand upon her heart whenever Dorothy's merry
voice reached her ears; and she still looked at the little girl with
wonder that she could find anything to laugh at.

THE WONDERFUL WIZARD
OF OZ.
L. FRANK BAUM, 1900

DOROTHY, RISING

DOROTHY, RISING, LOOKS OUT THE window and gasps. There are trees out there in the open air, their roots twirling through the sky like tassels. There are clods of earth, pieces of tin from the roof of a house, reflecting in the fractured light. There's a wagon wheel, spinning, just like the house Dorothy rides within, and then the floor shifts beneath her and she stumbles, one hand placed against the floor in haste to brace herself as she falls and scrapes her knees.

The cyclone had arrived in the blink of a moment: Uncle Henry had run off to tend to the cattle in the shed, Aunt Em had scurried down the trap door into the dark hole of the cellar like a practiced rodent, and then the wind came and picked the house up like Dorothy picks up Toto, her darling black dog with little eyes like chips of coal. In one swift scoop, the house was lifted into the sky above Kansas; and then, from up there, Dorothy could see Uncle Henry peeking over the front gate of the barn to watch his home swirl up into the gray curdling clouds above. She could see Aunt Em slowly stand from her frightened crouch in the now wide-open cellar. She could see Aunt Em reach out her hand, as if she might grab hold of Dorothy's outstretched fingers and pluck the girl out of the swirling air, as if she might pull Dorothy back down to earth at the last moment.

But it is too late for escapes. The house is up in the sky, far too high for anyone to pull Dorothy back down to the gray fields of Kansas. And the cyclone itself only continues to lift the house higher and higher, spinning it like a top.

Dorothy holds Toto under one arm, pulls her other hand away from the window where she had stretched it out toward Aunt Em's tiny figure in the cellar, which now looks like a hole in the earth, an open grave where someone might eventually be buried. She can't see Aunt Em any longer. She can't see Uncle Henry, or the shed, or the outlines of their property, or the copse of trees where she likes to go in summer to hide beneath their shade and pretend she's a fairy princess who lives in a forest, the scent of pinecones following her every step. She does see a pig through the window, though, and then a chicken, and then a cow. They go whirling around outside, caught up in the cyclone's spinning, and Dorothy puts her fingertips to her pink lips again, hoping to hold in another gasp.

Toto struggles under her arm, wriggling like a small child, and Dorothy drops him. The dog immediately starts yapping, circling the floor of the one-room house over and over, as if he has lost his favorite toy. Without thinking about the consequences of giving the dog his freedom, Dorothy is stunned as she watches him run toward the open trap door that Aunt Em had fled through moments ago, down into the cyclone cellar. Toto peers down into the open space, barks at the arms of the cyclone lifting the house up through the sky, as if the cyclone might listen to the anger of a small canine. Then, to Dorothy's surprise, Toto throws himself through the hole.

"Toto, no!" Dorothy screams at the little black dog that made her gray days in Kansas a bit happier. She runs to the center of the room, worrying that she'll see the dog falling through the sky below her, a nightmare image that she's already sure will come to haunt her, should she somehow survive. When she runs over to the edge of the trap door to look, though, Toto is hovering in midair directly below the space he fell through, only inches below the opening. He is held up by the invisible hands of the cyclone. It has rejected him.

Toto whimpers, and Dorothy plunges her arms through the opening to pull him back into the house with her. She slams the trap door shut, slides its bolt into place so that it won't fly open again, then says, "Bad, Toto. Bad dog."

Toto licks her face in gratitude, a wet pink tongue in a black face, one of the few pieces of color that kept Dorothy going throughout her gray, gray childhood, where Uncle Henry joylessly tilled the gray fields with his plow and Aunt Em seemed to always be hanging their gray laundry out to dry.

Up and up and up the house goes, born up by the cyclone, which is at the very center where the north and the south winds meet. The house occasionally tips from side to side in a sleepy rhythm, its planks creaking, rocking Dorothy into a lull, as if she were a baby being rocked in a cradle by its mother. Dorothy wouldn't know anything about mothers taking care of a baby though. She was an orphan who Uncle Henry and Aunt Em had taken in after she'd already started to stumble across floors on her own. She can't remember the orphanage she came from very well, but she does remember that it was a dark-roomed place with windows that seemed to glow, and that she had a small cot under one of those windows, and that sunlight came in under the blind each morning, rolling across her legs and chest until it reached her face and warmly lifted her eyelids.

Her eyelids feel heavy now, though, and her skin is cold. Between the swaying of the house and the strange quiet at the center of the cyclone, it makes her drowsy. Which is odd, she thinks, considering how she should really be afraid. When the cyclone eventually disperses, the house will fall—she knows this—and she will die when it returns to the earth below with a resounding crash. How far away from Aunt Em and Uncle Henry would she land? she wonders. Would they ever find the remains of their house? Would they find Dorothy and Toto buried within its rubble? Or would the last thing they ever saw of her be her hand stretching toward them from the window, reaching out, grasping at air?

Dorothy pushes aside her questions, which are far too difficult for a girl of her age to contemplate. And besides, the house continues to travel up through the sky, higher and higher, past the clouds that appear now and then at a window. In fact, Dorothy is suspicious about something. When she looks through the windows now, there is no gray sky at all. A blackness full of pinholes of light, winking and blinking at her, has grown around her. And the roaring of the wind has slowly but surely begun to subside. A soft purr surrounds the house now, bolstering it on its journey. And the air seems thin. So thin, Dorothy finds herself gasping for breath on occasion, as if it's in short supply.

She feels woozy, as if the clouds have come inside the house and drifted into her head. She could go to sleep, if she let herself, which Dorothy thinks she should do. Besides, what can she do about anything anyway? The house has left earth behind. The house has left the sky behind, the clouds behind. The stars are her destination. Dorothy has no one to count on, other than Toto. This is something that could easily bother her, considering her past, considering she had no mother or father and only could piece together a vague narrative of how she came to be in the orphanage in the first place. She's heard Uncle Henry say things when he didn't realize she was standing in the doorway. She's heard Aunt Em say, "The child, Hank," in reply to Uncle Henry's remarks about Dorothy's mother and father. And from what she's gathered, her father was "a no good sonuvabitch," and that his sister—Uncle Henry's sister, that is—would have been rolling in her grave to know what a failure her husband had been after all she went through to bring that little girl into the world. Dorothy couldn't understand everything Uncle Henry said in his occasional uproars (they usually came on him when he drank too much of his bathtub gin, as Aunt Em called it). But she did understand that Uncle Henry and Aunt Em had done her a great favor. As she'd once heard Aunt Em say, "If it weren't for us, that child would have no one."

Dorothy has no one now, she thinks, except for Toto. She keeps reminding herself that she's lucky enough to have him with her, though. Now that she's battened down the cyclone cellar hatch, he's quieted and has curled up at her feet like the good dog that he usually is.

The house shakes slightly: a faint rumble that disappears as quickly as it came. Dorothy sits down on the cot in the corner—her cot. Uncle Henry's and Aunt Em's bed is still lodged across the small room in its corner. The house is really too small for it to be called a house—even the orphanage where Dorothy started life out was bigger than this place—but Dorothy implicitly understood when she came here that this shack (what it looked like, really) was something Uncle Henry and Aunt Em took pride in. It was "theirs." They said so, over and over. They said how hard they were working for it, as if the house (shack) were their employer. They sent money to the bank every month to pay for it. The way Uncle Henry worked, Dorothy was surprised they didn't already own it. He came in from the fields when the sun went down, and was gone from the house (shack) each morning before Dorothy woke. She looks around after the walls rumble, and wonders, *Maybe you were worth more than I thought. After all, you're still here. With me. With Toto.*

What Dorothy doesn't know right now, though, is possibly more important than anything else that's occurring around her. The house she is slowly but steadily beginning to grade at a higher value will crash land on an alien world several hours later. It will have served her well, yes. And she will then go through a dangerous journey to return herself to Uncle Henry and Aunt Em by way of a road of yellow bricks that will lead her to an emerald city, where she will discover how to transport herself back into the waiting arms of her adoptive parents. They will go on to build a new house in place of this one, and later, after much toil—after much back-breaking toil—Uncle Henry will lose that house to foreclosure. Men in black suits and tight ties will take it from him. This house and the other one in his and Aunt Em's future are never really "theirs" as much as they think so. This is a practice that, unfortunately, will not be indicative of their own particular placement in time and space in the United States at the turn of the century, but will continue on for years. Decades and decades and decades later, men in black suits and tight ties will still be taking homes away from hardworking people.

But right now, Dorothy is thankful for the house that hasn't abandoned her on this journey. A journey that she's still unable to comprehend is only the first leg, a journey that will soon be upon her like a lion, like a tiger, like a bear springing out of the woods beside her.

Dorothy lies back on her cot and stares up at the ceiling, where some of the plaster has fallen away to reveal the rafters. The roof has still held, though, thankfully. If it were to blow off, all would be lost. But right now, as the house shuttles through the column of darkness that surrounds it, Dorothy is thinking about her motion upward. About how it feels to rise and rise, endlessly, it seems, to rise higher and higher. It is much easier to fall, thinks Dorothy. There's an end, there is always an end. There is always a resounding crash, or else the surprising relief of something bringing one to a harmless halt before being hurled against the bottom of something. But rising is a different story. There is no bottom, just an upwardness that has no end in sight.

Dorothy closes her eyes. Finally, she drifts off into a pleasant slumber. Toto curls up at her side. In a few hours, she will wake again. The house will have settled down on its new world with a decidedly loud *thwump!* Then Dorothy will open her eyes, blinking like a doll, and her future will await her. A journey down the road of yellow bricks. Arriving at the City of Emeralds. The facedown with a witch. The magic held in the heels of her silver shoes.

Later, much later, after she discovers the magic trick that will return her to Kansas, Uncle Henry will lose his next house, not to a cyclone but to a mortgage, and Dorothy will take up her duties as a good daughter. She will come home and take Uncle Henry and Aunt Em out of their poverty and move them into a small farmhouse in the suburbs of the City of Emeralds. Dorothy herself will have a smart little apartment in the city itself, so she can take the train out to visit them very easily, where they can barbeque on their back deck and grill kebobs and drink wine in the evening. Dorothy will have become quite the celebrity in the city by that point—she will be best friends with the princess, they will appear in all of the best fashion magazines on their way to only the best parties in the City of Emeralds, and they will share secrets with each other like they were still sweet sixteen—so the house in the suburbs will serve as a good getaway during those times when she's feeling like the city is overwhelming her. And when she goes out to visit them, Dorothy will be able to see how she's given her aunt and uncle a decent end to their lives, there in the place where the cyclone that destroys her youth deposited her.

But right now she is blinking in the sunlight of that other world, adjusting her eyes to the future, beyond the gray wall of her childhood in Kansas, where her aunt and uncle must be tearing their hair out about her, wondering where she is, wondering if she has somehow survived this disaster. Right now, she is rising from her cot to walk across the floor of the house (shack), where she places her small hand on the knob of the front door. She twists the knob, and trembles a little as she twists it, anxious about what she will find on the other side of this motion she's taking.

Voices cry out to her from the other side of the door. Voices like she's never heard in her young life. Voices that are welcoming her ascendance.

Dorothy opens the door. She welcomes the light.

Peter called, "Mother! Mother!" but she heard
him not; in vain he beat his little limbs against the iron
bars. He had to fly back, sobbing, to the Gardens, and he
never saw his dear again. What a glorious boy he had meant
to be to her. Ah, Peter, we who have made the great mistake,
how differently we should all act at the second chance. But
Solomon was right; there is no second chance, not for most of
us. When we reach the window it is Lock-out Time. The iron
bars are up for life.

PETER PAN IN
KENSINGTON GARDENS.
J.M. BARRIE. 1906

THE BOY
WHO GREW
UP

IT WAS IN THE PARK I met him, one summer day when my Dad and I were
fighting (again) and I left (again), slamming the door behind me after
realizing I wouldn't be winning (again), and took the tube to Kensington
Gardens, where sometimes you can meet interesting people if the timing
and other magical aspects of the world are right. When I was angry, which
is what I'd been most of the time since my mum left a couple of years ago,
I'd always go to the gardens. Back when I was little, she used to tell me that
fairies lived there, that the flowers in the beds were actually their disguises. I
never believed her, really—and after she left I thought of that as just another
example of her tendency to lie—but by the time the sun went down that day,
I'd see hundreds of them. Fairies, that is. And him too. Peter.

He wasn't what I expected, though I hadn't really gone to the
gardens expecting to see him in the first place. And anyway, what can you
truly expect from someone you thought was a character out of a story
adults read to children?

That's what my mum used to do. She'd read to me from this one book about Peter. Not the famous one with Wendy and Neverland, but the one where Peter was first introduced, *The Little White Bird*. That was back when she still wanted to be part of our family. That was back before she met Marcus the Carcass Splitter, owner of the absurdly posh butcher shop called *Chop Chop* over in Camden Town. That was back before she left my dad and me behind for bloody fat-marbled sides of beef.

In the stories my mum used to read, Peter always seemed like a perpetual ten-year-old, but the Peter who stood in front of me that day, admiring his own statue (which looked like the little kid version of him) seemed more round my age. Fifteen or sixteen. Reddish-brown hair sticking up like he'd just pulled his head off a pillow. Wearing this costume of a leaf-covered vest and soft leather pants. And boots, too, up to the tops of his calves.

I didn't realize who he was right away. I thought he was just another nutter, or someone really into cosplay, or maybe just this huge fan of Peter Pan who'd gotten a bit carried away. But none of that put me off him. He was exactly the sort of person I'd hoped I'd come across. Someone lost, someone looking for something that might Change Things.

I'd been there for about twenty minutes before he showed up, but no one really interesting had come by. Just mums and dads with kids, tourists clicking the camera buttons on their phones. So I'd kept my hands in my pockets and kept walking, hoping someone right would eventually meet my eyes. The world seemed to conspire against me that day, though, and I began to worry I'd end up back at our flat feeling the same way I had when I left.

Then suddenly he was just there, standing next to the Peter statue like he'd been beamed down to earth from his alien world past the second star to the right and straight on until morning. And for the first full minute after he materialized, all he did was stand there and stare at that statue of himself like he was looking up at Christ on the cross or something.

"You like him?" I finally said, grinning as I interrupted him pondering the statue like someone absorbed in one of their own selfies. I lifted my chin in the direction of the statue and chuckled a little, trying to put him at ease, but he only turned to me with this squint in his eye and said, "It's been so long since I've been that little."

I couldn't stop myself from snorting. Clearly the kid was messing with me. But when his face didn't budge, I squinted back and said, "You lose your way from the hospital or something?"

"This was the spot," he said, utterly serious, and pointed at the stump-like pedestal the bronze Peter statue stood on, which had these stone fairies etched into its base, fanning their wings as they looked up at him like some kind of god. "This was the spot where I landed after I flew out my window and the bird Solomon told me I was more human than I thought, and that humans can't fly. And because he said that, I fell and landed. Right here."

"Are you for real?" I asked, and he just blinked and nodded like, of course. I nodded back, just once, thinking, *Right, this is going to be interesting*. Even if the kid was a complete liar or just out of his mind in general, or maybe doing performance art of some kind, I liked that he believed in what he was trying to sell me.

"I had a boat too," he said, "right over there," and he pointed toward a group of trees that lined the river. "I used to stash it there when I came across the Serpentine from the island where Solomon's bird friends built me the boat from mud and twigs."

"Come on," I said, "Let's have a look then."

"At the boat?" he said, raising his eyebrows.

I nodded and smiled, encouraging him to keep the game going. Of course he'd back down after I pushed for proof, I figured, because there really wasn't any. "Yeah," I said. "The boat. Let's go for a sail in it, why don't we?"

"It's probably fallen apart by now," he said, shaking his head in resignation. And I thought, *Here it comes*. "But if it's anywhere," he said as he turned again toward the copse of trees by the river, "it would be there." He looked over his shoulder at me then and said, "You do believe me, don't you?"

"Yeah," I said, shrugging. "Why wouldn't I?" And hearing that, he seemed to brighten a bit, to stand up straighter, and then he grinned like a fool.

"Let's go then!" he said, suddenly sounding like a little kid calling out the start of a surprise race, and then he turned to sprint in the direction of the tree line. "Beat you there!"

Nutter, I thought, shaking my head as I watched him go. *Utter nutter.* But I ran off a second later, laughing a little because I'd gone this far with him already, running to look for a non-existent boat made out of twigs and mud. I figured it was better than being at home pretending like my dad and I weren't ready to commit acts of immense violence upon each other.

When I caught up to him down by the banks of the Serpentine, he was standing half-bent over, looking at something. And when I came to a stop beside him, I couldn't believe what I saw.

A nest. A big nest. A human-sized nest, really, had been pulled up on the bank of the river. It was covered with moss and some fallen branches and a few vines that had grown around it over time, camouflaging it from ordinary passersby. Peter looked up with a glint in his eye. "I told you," he said. "I told you it'd be here if it was anywhere. Get in."

"Are you mad?" I said. "That boat's not big enough for both of us. We'll go down like the bloody Titanic."

He laughed like he thought I'd told a joke, slapped one of his thighs like he was doing a pantomime play of Peter Pan, and suddenly I started to wonder if maybe one of those was actually going on in the park that day and he'd somehow escaped from the venue, gone off the rails, threw the script over his shoulder, and this group of children were just then sitting in a semi-circle somewhere asking their mums when Peter was going to come back and finish the story.

"You're funny," he said. "I like that. Not everyone can tell a proper joke." Then he cleared away the branches and vines and pushed the boat out into the water, wading next to it. "It'll be fine," he said. "Come on already."

I waited for him to get in the boat, which bobbed on top of the water even after it held his weight inside it. There was barely room in there for me, but he held his hand out anyway, curled his fingers inward a couple of times. I thought about those fingers for a second, the way they might feel on my skin, and shivered.

"It isn't going to work with both of us in there," I said. I put my hands in my pockets and looked back toward the Peter statue, ready to run. The light was starting to turn this greyish-purple color, as if whole hours had burned away in the last five minutes, and the grounds looked incredibly empty where just seconds before hordes of people had been milling.

Then I heard a *clang, clang, clang* sound coming from all sides of the park, and Peter whispered in the most alarmed way, "It's Lock-out Time. We must hurry."

"Are you saying we've been locked in?"

"No," said Peter. "I'm saying humans have been locked out. Hurry. The fairies will be coming soon, and you're not a baby. They like human babies, but not grown-ups."

"I have a mobile with me," I said, and fished my phone out. But when I started tapping on the keypad, I got nothing. No numbers. No bars. No anything. "What the?" I said, tapping and tapping.

"There's no time for whatever that is," said Peter. "Hurry. Get in."

So I stashed my phone in my pocket and waded out into the water—because what else could I do, really—and climbed into that nest of a boat to squeeze in beside him.

❦

IT WAS A PRETTY MESSED up idea, but my life was pretty messed up right then. I didn't want to go home to my dad and have to apologize for the argument we'd had earlier, during which I'd called him the biggest wanker in the world, and then proceeded to tell him how I wished he and my mum had never had me. Sitting in a nest-like boat seemed somehow more preferable.

Peter didn't say much as we floated down the Serpentine. He just slipped a small garden spade from between two branches in the nest and held it up in the air, where it gleamed under the moonlight. I blinked a few times, then gasped as I realized the moon was already out and shining down on the spade and on the rippling water. "My old paddle," said Peter, waving it around like a sword.

"It's a garden spade," I pointed out.

"I *know* that," he said, rolling his eyes. "I just didn't know it back then, when I was only seven days old."

"You paddled down the Serpentine in this nest with a garden implement when you were seven days old?" I said, blinking over and over. I couldn't manage to keep the scorn out of my voice, or the roll out of my eyes.

Peter nodded. "I also used it to bury the children."

My throat constricted, hearing that, and the sudden urge to throw myself overboard came on me. "You buried *children?*"

"The ones who got lost," Peter replied like this was quite normal.

"Lost?" I said, thinking maybe I should have just gone back home and apologized after all.

"Yes," said Peter. "They'd either get lost on their way to their mothers after hatching, or on their way back when they decided they wanted to be birds again instead of humans."

"Okay, this has gone on long enough," I said, and tried to wriggle away from him, to put some space between our bodies. But the nest-boat was too small. Our shoulders were pressed together, his right knee knocked against my left, and he rested one elbow on my chest as he held the spade up over my head like it was bloody Excalibur. If he hadn't been acting like such a little kid, which was a huge turn-off, I might have slid my hand under his tunic to see if he were up for it.

"No," he said. "We haven't gone far enough to reach the island yet." Then he turned to the side and dipped the spade into the dark water and began to paddle.

I didn't know what to do other than sit there and grill myself for being so flipping stupid. What had I been thinking? My dad would be wondering where I was. He might have even called my mum to ask if I'd shown up there, which would never happen, but if he was worried enough, he'd phone her. When I got home—*if* Peter didn't turn out to be a bloody serial killer and I *did* get to go home—my dad would annihilate me for running off again, which is something I'd been doing for the past year, whenever we had a row. I hated this idea I had right then, as I drifted in the nest-boat, this idea that the last thing I might ever hear my dad say was, "Colin, I'm sorry, but shouting at me and running off to who knows where isn't going to bring your mum home. She has a new home now, much as you don't like it."

She'd left when I was thirteen, right after she gave my dad her parting words. *Jonathan Crowe*, she had told him, *you are all mouth and no trousers*. Then she picked up the bags she'd packed before my dad got home from cabbying and walked out the door. Didn't look back, not even to catch my eye. She'd already been seeing Marcus the Carcass Splitter behind our backs for several months already. Had kept it a secret. She went to stay with Marcus then, and after the divorce, she got remarried within a few weeks, like we'd never meant anything.

I wanted to hate her. A lot. I did hate her, actually. But I couldn't keep hating her so hard forever, my dad kept saying. So I tried to forgive her instead. And sometimes I'd get to this place where I'd want to be around her again, because I missed her voice as she talked back to the wankers who populated her favorite talk shows on the telly, and I missed the sound of her whistling as she made us tea. And then, when she'd call or email to see how I was doing, I'd be decent enough to her, which was a mistake because then she got the idea that it was time to have me over for dinner with her and Marcus. I tried that a few times, but it never worked out. As soon as I'd knock on their door and she answered, saying, "Colin, my love!" and Marcus would come to stand behind her, all smarmy and grinning over her shoulder, I'd start hating her all over again.

It was because of what she'd said before she left—not to my dad, but to me, even though she didn't mean for me to hear—it was because of what she said that I couldn't forgive her.

❧

THE BOAT KNOCKED AGAINST LAND and Peter rolled against me, which was perfect timing, actually, because I'd been getting worked up thinking

151

about my mum. His body rolling against mine was a good remedy for anger, and I put my hands around his waist and winked. "We're here," he said, his stupidly smiling face so close to my own I could have kissed him. Instead I asked where *here* was. "Home," said Peter. "The place we all come from."

"Let's make it quick then," I said, losing interest since he wasn't showing any in my hands being on him. "I really need to be going."

Peter furrowed his brow. "You won't be going anywhere until morning when they open the gates," he said. When I gave him a look to pierce that stupid smile of his, he pulled back and said, "Well, maybe Solomon can help you. Maybe you can fly out. *If* you can remember how to fly, that is."

"I can't *remember* how to fly," I said, "because I've never flown before."

"Oh, but you have," said Peter. "Back when you were a bird."

I sighed instead of cursing. It was useless trying to reason with him. He was a character from a children's story. He was a child himself, trapped in a teenager's body.

We pulled the boat ashore to the cries of what sounded like a million night birds being disturbed, honking and chirping and cheeping or shrieking at our sudden presence. But when Peter lifted his hands and spread his fingers, they all fell silent. "Hello again!" he shouted into the blackness.

And all of the birds in unison said, "Peter!"

There was a great flurry of activity then, and I tried to stand behind him and not call attention to myself because honestly, I wanted to pretend this was all a dream, that I was really asleep at the base of the Peter Pan statue in the park. But the birds, unfortunately, wouldn't let me be. They kept circling round and landing, cocking their heads at me and asking Peter things like, "Who's this then, Peter? Another of your lost boys?"

"I'm not lost," I said, getting a bit tetchy. "I've just been locked in."

"Lost," one of the birds said. A thrush, I think. I shot it a look and it ruffled its feathers.

"Where's Solomon?" Peter asked once they'd all quieted.

"With the eggs, of course," said one of the birds. "He's got a very long list of expectations to fill, as usual."

"Come on, then," said Peter, looking at me. "Solomon will know what to do with you."

"I don't need anything done with me," I said.

"You need to get out, you said, *right now*, you said. Right?"

I nodded.

"Well, then," said Peter. "Solomon will know if that's possible."

WE WALKED TO THE CENTER of the island, where one particular tree grew taller than the others, and underneath it were rows of nests where birds sat on top of their eggs. Some of the birds grew startled at our approach and sent up a flurry of caws, then flew off into the night, leaving their eggs behind, some of which began to tremble. Cracks ran through several of them, beaks pierced through the openings, and suddenly there were these baby birds shrugging off flakes of shell like dogs shake off water. The baby birds looked back and forth between Peter and me as if one of us must be their mother. Then a gravelly voice boomed down from the canopy of the tallest tree. The voice shouted a series of numbers and street names, some of which I recognized, one in particular an address just round the corner from my mum and Marcus's flat. As the addresses were listed, the baby birds stretched out their wings, one after the other, and flew into the night sky like sparks from a bonfire.

"What—" I said. But I didn't really know how to follow through with that question.

"They're going to their mothers," said Peter.

"Their mothers are here," I said, looking at the empty nests where they'd been before we'd scared them. "Well, they *were* here, at any rate."

"They're going to their *human* mothers," said Peter. "You did it once, too. Don't look so horrified!"

Just then a stiff wind blew our hair back and a large crow circled the air above. After it landed between our feet, the crow looked up and said, "Peter, my Betwixt and Between, you've returned to us. And you've brought a friend, I see."

"I didn't mean to," Peter said. "I meant it to just be me, Solomon. Why are you still in charge here anyway? Last time I saw you, you said you had your eye on a tree over in the figs and planned to retire."

"My stocking of savings was stolen!" cried Solomon. "A hundred and eighty crumbs! Thirty-four nuts! Sixteen crusts! A pen-wiper and a bootlace! Everything gone! Everything! I couldn't retire after that. I've had to stay on!"

"That's terrible," said Peter, shaking his head in commiseration.

"It is," said Solomon, nodding. "Such is the way of the world, these days. A bird must work until his life expires. All of the mothers encourage their hatchlings to become human babies because of it, of course. Now for you, then. Why are *you* here?"

"I just came to see if everything was still the same," said Peter. "I suppose I was missing the place a bit."

"Caught in the webs of nostalgia?" Solomon said, chuckling. He flew up and landed on Peter's shoulder, so that he could look him straight in the eye. Peter crooked his head to the side to make room for him. "You've grown quite a bit since last we saw you. I didn't think you'd ever be able to grow up like a normal human child."

"Up there," said Peter as he looked up at the sky, "it's possible. Not like a normal human would grow, of course. Much slower. But at least I'm not a baby any longer."

Solomon turned to look where Peter was looking. So did I. And just then a star winked at us as if it had noticed us staring. "Even I haven't flown that far before," said Solomon. "It's quite wonderful to think of it, it is."

"It *is* a wonderful thought, isn't it?" said Peter. Then he turned back to Solomon and said, "My friend here needs to get out tonight. Can you help him?"

"Can he fly?" Solomon asked, looking at me past the bridge of Peter's slightly freckled nose.

"Of course not," said Peter. "Have you lost your marbles? He's human."

"*Quite* human," said Solomon, as if that were something you wouldn't want to be, really. "Quite human, indeed. But *you* relearned how to fly despite being part human, Peter."

"I can't fly," I said, interrupting them. "Really, I can't. And I don't think I'm going to be able to learn how to as early as tomorrow morning."

"You'll have to stay overnight then," said Solomon. "Peter can take care of you, I trust. He always took good care of the lost children he found in the park if they hadn't already died before he found them."

"Brilliant," I said, and sighed as I turned to start trudging back down the path we'd taken. "Just brilliant."

❦

"WHAT'S THE MATTER WITH YOU?" Peter asked as he slid his garden spade through the water again, paddling us back up the Serpentine a bit later.

"I just want to go home," I said. I was looking up at the stars, trying to not be angry and trying to not feel stupid for feeling like a kid about to cry because everything seemed so futile. Getting out of here seemed futile. My family seemed futile. *I* felt futile. I just wanted someone to hold onto, and Peter wasn't the someone I'd hoped to find that evening.

"I know what it means to want to go home," said Peter. "I flew out of my mother's window when I was seven days old and when I tried to go back she'd already had another child. And even now, after making a home up there, I know what it feels like to miss other homes. Kensington Gardens was my first, you know, not up there. But you've been steam-out-the-ears and arms-folded like you're a statue since I met you." He paddled a couple more strokes, then looked at me, very shocked, as if he'd been startled. "Are you a statue from the gardens come to life?" he asked, as if that would explain my stiffness.

"What are you on about?" I said, snorting at the idea. "I'm not a bloody statue. Your head is broken."

"No it's not," said Peter. "I'd know if I had a broken head. I lost my shadow once and I knew it when that happened, so I'd know if my head were broken as well."

I rolled my eyes. "Enough," I said, and slid a cupped hand into the water to help him paddle faster.

When we approached the spot we'd set off from though, Peter pulled his spade up and stopped paddling. "What's wrong?" I asked, still scooping handfuls of water on my side of the nest-boat. I wasn't giving up so easily.

"The fairies will be waiting for us," Peter said gravely. "And they haven't seen me in a long while. They may not recognize me. I'm not a child any longer. They may want to kill us."

"*Kill us?*"

"Well, you more so than me. I should be okay if they do recognize me. They're very adamant about keeping humans out of the gardens after Lock-out Time," said Peter. "The only thing that saved me from them the first time I rowed up to their shore was that I was still a baby and all the women-fairies wanted to take care of me once they saw that. Even fairy women love human babies."

I wanted to tell him love for babies is far too easy. My mum proved that. I wanted to tell him about how my mum didn't give a shit about me after I wasn't a baby and took off when she didn't like who I was becoming. I wanted to say, "You know what? While my mum was telling off my dad in the next room, right before she left us, she told him it was probably because my dad was such a weakling wanker that his son had become a poof." A poof. A bleeding poof is what she'd called me that day.

Thanks, Mum. Thanks a lot.

Being abandoned as a baby like Peter might have been easier than growing up with a mum who didn't like who her baby boy grew up to be, like I did. But I didn't put that thought to Peter. We didn't need to compete about who'd had it worse, I figured. We could both feel like our early lives sucked and maybe we'd both gotten stuck in those places precisely because of how sucky they were.

Despite the fact that we'd stopped paddling, the boat continued to drift toward the riverbank, and as we grew closer, I began to see them. Little people with pointed ears and fanciful clothes of so many different colors came out of the shadows. Seeing that, I realized why my mum used to say they hid themselves away dressed as flowers. I smiled at that thought, then frowned in the next instant. I was thinking of her again, and thinking of her made me mad all over.

When the boat landed, bumping up against the bank and jolting me out of my thoughts, it turned out that the fairies didn't try to kill us after all. Instead they sent up a great cheer as Peter leapt from the boat into their waiting arms, surrounding him like fireflies, their many wings all aflutter, covering him with kisses like a hero returned home from war.

After all the pomp and circumstance, though, it was mostly a disappointment, to be honest. Peter seemed to forget about me, and the fairies were so caught up in his return that they didn't notice me in the slightest. They all moved off from the banks of the Serpentine together, back into the gardens, where they began to play music and pass tiny cups of wine down the lines of their tiny tables and dance and sing like it were a holiday party. One of them—their queen, I figured from all of the lining up and bowing that went on around her—gave Peter a set of pipes, which he started to play at her request, and then they all twirled along the garden paths together, drunk and laughing like idiots.

I kept my distance. To be honest, I was relieved they had no interest in me, and I was also starting to get tired of dealing with Peter. There was something off about him. I mean, he was exactly as described in the books about him—always stoked for endless adventure—but I wasn't so charmed as I'd been when I was little and his storybook life seemed like a thing I would have given anything to have. Now, being so close to him, I felt more like, I don't know, like he had something *wrong* with him. He unnerved me.

I sat down at the base of the Peter statue instead of following after. Rested my back against the bronze stump, gathered my knees into my arms, checked my phone again. When it still showed nothing but a grey screen, dead as dead can be, I tilted my head back to look up at the stars wheeling above.

There it was, the second star on the right, winking at me, as if it were giving me an invitation to move there. I looked down though, stared at my untied shoelaces and thought about other things. Mum, mostly, even though I didn't want to. She would have a good laugh if I ever told her about this evening.

Time passed. The color of the sky changed, lightening ever so slightly as morning made its way back. I didn't sleep. I just sat there and tried to think about what I'd say to my dad when I was able to go home again. He'd murder me, for sure. I wouldn't be going anywhere for a while. Curfew would be reinstated. I'd be living in my own personal dystopia. He'd probably even threaten to send me off to live with Mum and Marcus if I didn't settle down.

A shadow fell over me at some point, and I looked up to find Peter standing above me, blocking out the stars, which were beginning to fade as the sky lightened. "You've made it," he said. "You've spent a whole night in the gardens. Not many can say that. How do you feel?"

"How do I feel?" I said, and looked away. "I feel like an idiot."

"You're not an idiot," said Peter. He knelt on his haunches then, so he could look at me straight on.

"I'm so fucked up," I said, shaking my head.

"No," said Peter, "you're not."

"Yes," I said. "I am."

"How do you figure?"

"I think too much. Mum always said so. Her and my aunt Donna. My aunt Donna once said that my personality would ruin me. It was at some kind of family thing, I forget which one, and my mum was still around, so I wasn't able to say anything in return without getting a clout on the head by my dad for talking back. When we got home though, I asked my mum what aunt Donna had meant, and she said Donna didn't have a way with words, that was for certain, but that she thought she meant I thought too much. And that it would do me no good in life to give things that kind of attention."

"What do you think about that now?" Peter asked.

"I dunno," I said, shaking my head. "I guess she was right. My aunt Donna, I mean. I think about things too much. I think about my mum more than I should. I think about her more than she deserves. I wonder sometimes, is she thinking about me as much as I'm thinking about her? And then I think, *To hell with her. Stop caring, like she stopped caring about you.*"

Peter stood again, put his hands on his hips and said, "I tried to go back to my mother once, but she'd already had another child and she'd forgotten about me mostly. I know how you feel." He held his hand out then, and I looked at it for a moment, not sure what he wanted. It was far past the time to be looking for a rub. "You can come with me," he said, and I blinked a little before asking where.

"Back to where I'll be going" was his answer.

I looked up into his eyes and knew where he was talking about. I knew from the books my mum had read where he'd be going, where I could go if I just took his hand and let him fly me away from all my problems. Mermaids and pirates and eternal childhood. All of that and some fairy dust lingering in the air like snowflakes after.

"No, thanks," I said and sighed. I couldn't leave my dad, no matter how hard we were fighting, and for better or for worse, I couldn't leave my mum, even though what she'd said had flayed me and kept flaying me for these past two years. "I've got...I've got to get things right here, somehow," I said, thinking I would probably go over to my mum's place after the gates opened in a while, and I'd act really strange most likely, showing up out of the blue like that. But hopefully she'd make breakfast and maybe we could try to figure out how to talk to each other a little. "Maybe some other time though?" I offered.

Peter stared at me with those blank eyes of his—those eyes that could never get what human eyes understand as ours grow older and see more of the world, the good and the bad of it—and I shivered. No words passed between us after that, though we kept staring at each other like we were mirror images, or one of us a shadow come undone from the other, and we couldn't or at least didn't want to let go.

I almost reached out to him, but before I could, Peter turned away and transformed into a little white bird, which all of us are before we become human beings. And then he flew away, up into the pale morning sky studded with fading diamonds.

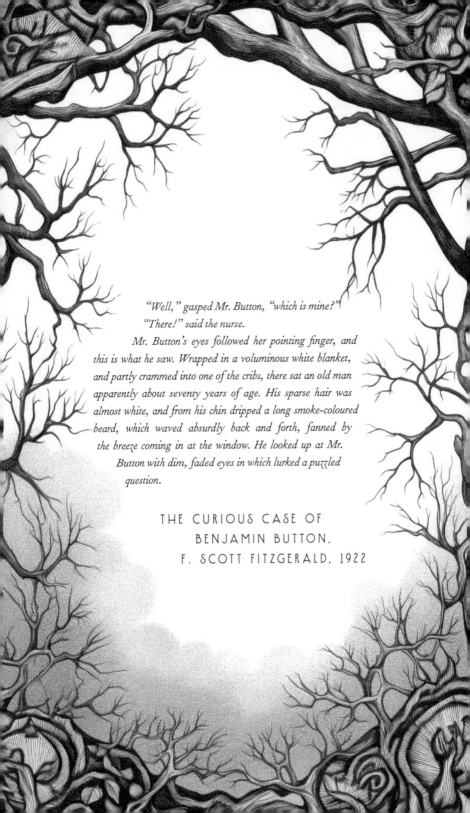

"Well," gasped Mr. Button, "which is mine?"

"There!" said the nurse.

Mr. Button's eyes followed her pointing finger, and this is what he saw. Wrapped in a voluminous white blanket, and partly crammed into one of the cribs, there sat an old man apparently about seventy years of age. His sparse hair was almost white, and from his chin dripped a long smoke-coloured beard, which waved absurdly back and forth, fanned by the breeze coming in at the window. He looked up at Mr. Button with dim, faded eyes in which lurked a puzzled question.

THE CURIOUS CASE OF
BENJAMIN BUTTON.
F. SCOTT FITZGERALD. 1922

THE 24 HOUR BROTHER

MY LITTLE BROTHER JOE GREW up too fast for his own good. My mom was the first to see what we were in for. Soon after Joe's birth, when the nurse put him in her arms, the first thing he did, still pink and slimy, was smile the gummy, wry smile of a little old man.

"Joseph, Joe, my baby boy," said my mother, "we'll try our best if you will." She kissed his cheek and handed him back to the nurse hastily, trying to keep herself from falling in love with someone who she realized, at their very first meeting, would only break her heart. The first sign was in that first smile: the old man Joe would soon become, the old man Joe would become too soon.

I was there for the birth, too. The midwife kept looking over her shoulder and saying, "Come look at this, Lewis! It's incredible!" but I shook my head. While Dad hovered over the bed with a video camera, I backed myself into a corner.

It was an important day, Joe's birthday. Fifteen years before, while my mother was giving birth to me, there'd been "complications." The doctor had told her it would be nearly impossible for her to have any more children. At Joe's birth, though, all that doctor could do was throw his hands in the air and look from nurse to midwife to mother, father, and finally to me. "It's a miracle!" he said. "It's a miracle, I'm sure!"

"Do you hear that, Lewis?" said my father. He paused in his recording of the event to look back at me in my corner. "A miracle. Come over and see your little brother."

For weeks my parents had been drilling me on the importance of being a big brother. I would be one of Joe's confidantes, I would be one of his guides. But I was frightened at the thought of all that responsibility. So when I saw Joe on his back, being weighed, waving his little limbs like an overturned insect, all my fears evaporated. I was able to smile for the first time in days. Face red and screaming, tiny body dimpled with white splotches, he looked so helpless that I knew right away I'd fill the shoes of a big brother better than anyone. "Joe," I whispered, stroking the backs of my fingers across his pasty cheek, "I'm your big brother. Lewis. Welcome home."

"What a lovely sentiment, Lewis," said my father. "Joe's very lucky to have you for a brother." He tousled my hair, hugged me to his shoulder, and lifted the recorder back up to his eye. "Smile," he said when the nurse gave Joe to my mom, the cord no longer dangling. Mom grinned then--a blinking, reluctant grin, still holding strong to the secret of what she'd seen before the rest of us had had a chance to notice--and held Joe up in the crook of her arms.

That's when we saw what later Mom would tell us she'd already witnessed. Staring into the camera like an attention-starved movie star, Joe pulled back his lips to reveal a single tooth, perfectly white, rising out of the pale pink of his gums, like a tiny tombstone.

❦

THE TOOTH WAS NOT THE only thing to tip us off about Joe, though. Not even an hour later we were chasing him through the hospital. He weaved through the legs of nurses and orderlies while my dad and I dodged the spinning bodies he left behind him. As he stumped and slapped his way down the hall bare-footed, the baby fat on his legs jiggling, he experimented with a mouthful of new consonants and vowels. An orderly pushed my mom in a wheelchair behind us, but refused to match the pace Joe had set. Mom put her hands over her face and cried to see Joe trying to leave when already we had so little time to get to know him. When we finally did catch him, he had climbed onto a chair and was stretching his arm up to press the down button at a bank of elevators. My father took hold of him then, but Joe only shrieked with laughter before he started to wriggle out of my father's hands.

"This is all my fault," my mother said through the bathroom door of her room as she got dressed to leave the hospital later. She knew the risks, the mix-ups in chromosomes courted by men and women of a certain age. But her tests had all come back normal. There'd been others born like Joe in recent years, but the doctor had told my parents not to worry, had said everything was proceeding as normal.

Through the door my dad said, "Honey, it is not your fault," but my mom only replied by letting out a solitary, mournful moan.

❧

IT WAS THE FIRST OF January, that day. Joe was a New Year's baby. Outside, long feathers of snow sifted down from the sky while Mom and I waited with Joe in the lobby for my dad to hail a taxi. Phones rang, and the tiled floor displayed the shoe prints of people who had come and gone all day. When my dad finally stopped a cab, he came back to wheel my mother out and help her into the back seat. And since Joe had already shown his inclination for running away, I decided to take his hand as we left the lobby. As soon as my hand landed on his, though, Joe wrenched away from me. "What are you *doing*?" he demanded.

"I'm your big brother," I explained. "I'm here to protect you." I was shocked and a little hurt, but despite that I reached for his hand once more.

Joe flinched as if I'd tried to hit him. He hid his hands behind his back and said, in a scornful voice, "Don't you worry about me, Lewis. I can take care of myself." Then he ran to the taxi, his little jumper already tight on his growing body, and Dad lifted him in.

"Hurry up, Lewis," my mother called from the back seat. "You're letting out all of the warm air."

I climbed in beside her and considered the strip of electrical tape covering a rip in the seat's vinyl. One end of the tape was detached, curled up in a spiral. I imagined the previous taxi passengers lifting and reapplying it throughout the day. I started to do the same.

"Where to?" asked the driver. Dad gave him our address, then the toll light shifted on like a pinball blinker, and as we pulled into traffic, Joe lifted his head from Mom's open blouse to let out an enormous belch before falling asleep, out in the world for the first time.

❧

BY THE TIME WE WERE halfway home, Joe had woken again and was staring out the cab window at the passing cat's cradles of iron bridges and the looming facades of old brownstones on our side of town. He pointed up and we followed his chubby finger to look where he was looking: a large bird, a hawk or a falcon, wings spread wide against the sky as it circled the river. "Do you like that?" Mom asked, looking down at Joe again.

"I like the way it spirals," Joe said. "The way it flies like a leaf on the wind."

"A poet," said my father as Mom wiped away a tear.

Dad carried Joe up the steps to our building like a bride over a threshold. Then up we went to the second floor to show Joe the room we'd spent the last nine months preparing for him. Now, though, we felt embarrassed. The room we'd made was for an ordinary newborn. Joe took the stuffed dinosaur from the toy box and looked up at the mobile of stars and moons dangling over his crib. He looked back then, frowning, and said, "Thank you. It's beautiful."

We didn't waste any more time making him comfortable. He was too big for everything, so Dad went out and came back an hour later with a truck full of new furniture. A twin bed, a desk and chair, a baseball glove, a baseball, a notebook in which Joe could write his poetry. After the movers took away all the baby things, Joe sat on his bed and jumped up and down, testing the springs. He took the baseball glove, tossed the ball in the air and caught it, then opened the notebook and wrote a haiku:

A bird on the wind
A ball in my leather glove
All is mystery.

MOM COOKED HER FAMOUS LASAGNA. Joe devoured it in minutes, then sat in front of the TV and watched a show about criminals being captured by the police. Dad asked Joe if we could do anything for him, and Joe, knees gathered under his chin, arms wrapped around his legs, turned and said, "I don't know. If there is, you'll have to tell me. I don't know what I need."

SO WE WENT TO THE store and bought clothes that fit him, jeans and sweaters, a winter coat, warm socks and boots to trudge through the snow like a trooper. Then we went to the park and looked at the pond frozen over, the icicles hanging from branches, then on to Fifth Avenue to skate at Rockefeller Center, Christmas music blaring, lights blurring as little kids fell over and older siblings righted them. Joe loved the clustered lights, the clustered people. He skated with swift determination, but didn't fall no matter how wildly he pumped his arms to pick up speed. He made friends with a little girl who, when we left, kissed him on the cheek and waved goodbye from the rink, her green-mittened hand held high over her head.

On the way home, Joe said he was hungry again and my mom said that that didn't surprise her, he was a growing boy and he was already outgrowing those clothes we'd just bought him. So we stopped at a Japanese place and ordered him fifteen kinds of sushi. When the bill came, Mom's eyes widened but Dad just shrugged, said it was nothing, really, that exposure to the cuisines of other cultures is an important thing, don't you think, and Mom could only nod with pursed lips while she raised her hand to order another cup of sake.

At home, Joe went to bed and we stood in the dark, not saying anything, just looking at him. At the frail lashes of his closed eyes and his boy's face changing minute by minute into the face of a young man. We couldn't sleep even though Joe was sleeping soundly. We could only stay where he was and watch him growing.

"Will he stop?" I asked after a while.

"No," said my dad, shaking his head, not looking at me.

"No, honey," said my mom, shaking her head, looking at me.

I turned back to Joe and stroked my fingers against his cheek like I'd done after he was born that morning. I thought about stop signs, red lights, crossing guards with whistles. Slow down, I thought. Slow down already.

I FELL ASLEEP AT SOME point, unable to keep my head from nodding, and was woken an hour later by the sounds of shouting and a door slamming. I sat up at the foot of Joe's bed, where I must have curled up as I drifted, but Joe wasn't in the room with me. Neither were my parents. A square of moonlight fell on the floor where I was sitting. I stood up and went out to the living room, where I found my mom on the phone, saying, "Eighteen or nineteen, maybe twenty. But in a while he'll look older. No, I don't have a picture." She paused then, looked up at the ceiling, tears already spilling, and said, "I don't have any pictures!"

Joe had run off again, given us the slip in the middle of the night, and my dad was out looking for him while my mother babbled uncontrollably to the police, who said they were on it, though they never did have the chance to find him. It was only a half hour later that my dad returned with Joe in tow, my dad's hand on Joe's meaty shoulder like a claw to steady him.

Joe weaved as he walked, as if he were still a toddler. He was taller than me now, and muscular. He wore clothes we'd never bought him: knee-ripped jeans, a tight T-shirt, a fake fur coat that hung down to his ankles. His hair was all spiked and he had lipstick lips on his neck and cheeks, where a five o'clock shadow was starting to cover him over. When my mom saw him, she screamed something incomprehensible, then ran over and took him into her arms. She pulled away a moment later, her face scrunched up, and sniffed at him. "Have you been drinking?" she asked, then looked at my father. "Has he been drinking?" she asked again, louder.

Dad had found Joe only two blocks away, at a dive bar, totally hammered. When we sat down in the living room and drank the hot tea Mom made for us, Joe cried and said, "I just didn't want to think about it anymore."

We nodded. We knew. We didn't want to think about it anymore either.

But it was inevitable that our thoughts circled back to what was happening right in front of us, the way Joe continued to change the rest of the night until the sun rose and he looked ready to pass up Dad in the Department of Graying. And then, by mid-morning, his skin had loosened and fell down like dress socks, as if he were ready to put on a worn-out suit and go to the park to sit on a bench feeding breadcrumbs to pigeons. His days as a barfly were over. Joe, Joseph, their son, my little brother, was getting ready to leave us.

JOE SLEPT ON THE COUCH until that afternoon, and we sat around watching his chest rise and fall with his breathing. At first, rhythmically: a steady lifting. Then, later, uneven: stuttering with the rise, stuttering with the fall. We sighed. We shook our heads or looked away altogether. I looked down at my feet, at the rug, until the rasping couldn't be heard any longer, and lifted my head when Mom got up to kneel beside Joe's age-wizened body, to hug him one last time.

His hair was long and white, rolling over his shoulders like an angel's, his face lined with wrinkles. His body was thin, curled in on itself like a question mark, his fingers long and bony. I tried to think of him as the baby who had got up on two legs the previous morning and run down the hospital hallways, screaming with laughter. But I couldn't remember him that way as long as I looked at who he was now.

Dad stood, too, bent down to kiss Joe on the forehead. Then he helped Mom to stand and, together, they called the hospital to tell them the time.

❧

I DIDN'T GO TO THE funeral, so I don't know what the minister said as they stood around his casket. I don't know who came to pay respects or who my parents chose to act as pallbearers. My dad had asked me, but I'd shaken my head, said I wasn't going. "But you're his brother. His big brother, Lewis," he said. "You have to."

I didn't, though. I couldn't. For twenty-four hours I'd had a brother, I'd watched him grow from child to man to end, to exit. That was enough for me. That was all I could take seeing. I didn't want to know any more of what came after. I stayed at home and played video games instead, drank too much soda, got a stomachache, stared out the window of my bedroom at a bird on a wire, snow falling around it, listened to music on my iPod, chatted online with a friend who knew nothing of what had happened to me over vacation. I thought about the school break being over in just another day, being surrounded by people my own age again suddenly. How alien we were now, I thought, even me. We had years to go, years to continue growing, to become strangers to each other over and over, until even we couldn't recognize ourselves anymore.

Maybe Joe was right. All is mystery. And for the rest of my life, or at least for the next twenty-four hours, I wouldn't be able to stand it, any of it, until I got up to go back to school again two mornings later, where, sitting down at my desk, a friend already leaning over to tell me something that had happened to him over winter vacation, I made myself finally, decisively, peacefully forget.

A trapeze artist—
this art, practiced
high in the vaulted
domes of the great variety
theaters, is admittedly one of the
most difficult humanity can
achieve—had so arranged his life that,
as long as he kept working in the same building,
he never came down from his trapeze by night
or day; at first only from a desire to perfect
his skill, but later because custom was too
strong for him. All his needs, very modest needs
at that, were supplied by relays of attendants who watched
from below and sent up and hauled down again in specially
constructed containers whatever he required. This way of
living caused no particular inconvenience to the theatrical
people, except that, when other turns were on the stage, his
being still up aloft, which could not be dissembled, proved
somewhat distracting, as also the fact that, although at such
times he mostly kept very still, he drew a stray glance
here and there from the public. Yet the management
overlooked this, because he was an extraordinary
and unique artist. And of course they recognized that
this mode of life was no mere prank, and that only in
this way could he really keep himself in constant practice
and his art at the pitch of its perfection.

FIRST SORROW.
FRANZ KAFKA, 1922

KAFKA'S
CIRCUS

WHEN KAFKA'S CIRCUS COMES TO town, any who desire admittance to that spectacle of suffering must approach the entrance alone, for there is only room for a solitary body to pass through the ancient turnstile, which creaks and flakes off rust as you push through. In the past, many have attempted to trick the gatekeeper into thinking that they've followed the rules and come alone, while in secrecy a friend or lover has walked just ahead or followed directly behind. No matter how hard they've tried to obscure the nature of their intimacy, though, once past the turnstile they find that, quite suddenly, they are alone. They look behind and are no longer followed. They look ahead and see nothing but the black and white striped tents and the gray iron bars of the cages, where the Hunger Artist, that sliver of a person, can be seen performing the last phase of his eternal act of disappearance (the finest moment if you are a connoisseur of sorrow). They move forward then, separated from their beloved forever.

I've not come to see the Hunger Artist today, however, so I pass by his cage without even giving him a brief glance. And while ordinarily I'd feel guilty for such bad manners, neglect is the exact condition under which the Hunger Artist delivers his most admirable performances. To go unrecognized is his great ambition. Without acknowledging his presence, I've done him the great honor of making him feel invisible.

This is just one of the many rituals at Kafka's circus you must enact if you wish to become more than a casual visitor. To work yourself into the fabric of the circus, to become one of the faces that permanently fill its rows and big top benches, you must learn the art of sublimation. And then, once learned, never veer from its dictates. To falter at the test of the turnstile or the Hunger Artist's cage would result in only one thing for someone attempting to become, or at least to pass as, a devotee of the circus: a firm escort back to the world you thought you were escaping.

I can't afford to be hauled back today, though, back to where I've come from. I've come to see the trapeze artist, again, if I can reach him. If he'll let me reach him.

Peter.

Even the whisper of his name makes me long to see him swinging. Swinging and spinning through thin air.

❧

PETER. MY OLD FRIEND. PETER. The boy my father always told me to stay away from. "He's not on the same path as you," the old man, a leaning tower of a figure, already crumbling throughout my childhood, would say whenever I mentioned Peter's name. And when I once asked Father what he meant by different paths, he said, "You are meant for better things."

Better things. Father's way of saying Peter's family were street sweepers and sideshow acts and thieves, that nothing good could ever come of Peter because of that.

And me? Us? Our family? We were certainly better, according to Father, despite the fact that we lived just a hair's breadth from the wrong side of the so-called tracks, and despite the fact that my school clothes were always worn at the knees and elbows. Father had climbed to a point in his life where he was a head clerk in a bank. And while the income wasn't enough to propel him to the heights he desired to reach, it was better than what his own father had accomplished before him, he always said. And of course, if Father had his way, I would climb higher than he had.

Father. He always wore a stiff, dark suit, and if you looked closely enough, you would find the threads fraying at his cuffs and collars. He smelled of cigars, which he could often be found smoking, the clouds from their burning ends enveloping him like a noxious fog. From within that fog, Father would bellow. He'd shout. At me, at the world, about anything, and without any apparent reason. He was often angry about money, the very thing he worked with, the thing that he could not get enough of, despite it passing through his hands every single day. Often, while wallowing in the feeling that he had reached an impasse in his own life and could not grasp hold of whatever his younger self might have once dreamed of, he'd hurl obscenities at me for merely existing.

I had no mother, you see. She had died bringing me into this dreadful world of cigar smoke and fraying cuffs and collars and the dark shadows of our small apartment in a location that just barely qualified us as human, according to Father. Once, Father even told me that had I died alongside my mother in childbirth, he would have been better off.

So, when I had come home from school chattering about a boy named Peter, and when Father promptly delved to discover more about Peter's family and their circumstances—*such as they are*, he said with a sneer—I knew nothing could be done to continue my friendship with Peter other than to no longer talk about him in front of Father.

Peter's mother was a house cleaner, and sometimes on weekends she'd set up a table on the street and sell odds and ends. Things the people of the homes she cleaned no longer wanted. His father was always gone, working as an acrobat in Kafka's circus, which traveled across the country and even further, into other countries, on a circuit that might only allow his father to be home with Peter and his mother twice or three times a year at most. Peter and his mother lived in two rooms, both filthy with poverty and despair, and yet she compelled Peter to go to school, even though she could have put him to work in the streets like so many other poor children. And after the school day was over, Peter would go to the trapeze rig, which was set up on the outskirts of town, to train to become a trapeze artist.

"My father said if I could get good enough at it, he might someday be able to bring me into Kafka's Circus."

It was after school one day, in fact, that Peter first showed me how to climb the ladder of the rig to the platform and grab hold of the fly bar, then push off over a net to experience my first ever feeling of flight.

That first time, I wobbled through the air, my body spinning back and forth so much I simply fell into the net below, bouncing up and down like a ball. But despite my fall, it was the closest thing to freedom I'd ever tasted. I remember, after falling that first time, bouncing on my back in the net, looking up into the blue cloudless sky, and laughing with a kind of pure joy I'd never felt my body create in response to anything.

And then Peter's body flying through the air above. How graceful he was, how lithe. He didn't twist in the air like I had. He cut through it like a bird. He swung on the trapeze bar for a while, gathering speed, before he eventually pulled his legs over the bar and dropped his arms and hands below his head, laughing and waving at me as I lay below him.

And then, finally, he dropped, landing in the net beside me, making both of our bodies bounce up and down again for a while, making my body produce that pure joyous laugh once more.

"That was amazing," I said, after we'd caught our breath. "I don't know how you can do all of that."

"My father taught me," Peter said. "And there are people here who keep showing me new things."

"I wish I could do it, too," I said, recalling my awkward but wonderstruck momentary flight.

"You can," said Peter, hair flopping over his eyes, grinning. "I'll teach you."

He did exactly that, too, teaching me what he knew, training me as he'd been trained. Training me again whenever he learned something new. And for the rest of our school years, regardless of the dark and narrow rooms we grew within, we'd push ourselves free, up and into the sky, where the light could finally reach us.

That is, until our school days ended, and our fathers determined what paths we'd tread next.

Mine pulled me into the sterile halls of the bank, pushing paper in a silent cell. And Peter's father…he eventually came to take Peter to join Kafka's Circus.

❧

AFTER PASSING ALL THE INITIAL tests near the entrance to the circus, I continue to the big top, which stands in the center of the grounds surrounded by smaller tents, where lesser acts are featured during breaks for star performers. And after entering that cave of shadows, I climb a set of stairs to seat myself up in the gallery that looks down on the main circle. This is always my preferred perch, high up where I can best see Peter, that solitary swinger, for it's him that I come to see, again and again. For the past year, after Peter left, and as the circus has moved farther away on its nomadic trails, I've followed, taking trains across the countryside to small forlorn towns on the edge of nowhere, wanting to gaze upon his figure swirling with grace through space forever, wanting only to meditate upon his whirling figure for one last time, I tell myself, if only I could bear to part ways with him.

I cannot part ways with him. I know this now. Otherwise, I would stop this constant returning.

Beside me, another spectator sits leaning forward, his elbows resting on the balcony ledge as he peers down. He's a regular here. I know this because I'm a regular here. Spectators such as us—those who attend so frequently as to be recognized immediately by the circus workers and those others who, like me, can't help but continue to visit—sometimes seem as much a part of Kafka's circus as its performers. It's as if our own acts—our own performances—deal in the watching of others. And sometimes it's as though, *through* us, new spectators are able to view the exhibitions with a keener insight than they themselves may have perceived without us watching.

But the act that draws the spectator beside me with such regularity is not the one that holds me here. No, this spectator, a young man with dreams floating like clouds across his blue eyes, comes for the lively young woman who always rides bareback on a rowdy horse. The horse is occasionally whipped into a frenzy by the ringmaster as the girl jumps through great hoops held aloft by the muscle-braided arms of strongmen, and always she lands ever so gracefully on her feet atop the horse afterward. Then the crowd will rise with such devout cries of awe that their clapping hands seem more like steam hammers, automatic and unending, a deafening applause.

Spectators like us are always divided creatures, I realize as I sit and wait for Peter to arrive. We look inward and outward at the same time.

As I sit, waiting, the spectator beside me tries to negotiate that place between his interior world and the one that spreads out before him. He leans further over the balcony ledge, watching the young woman wildly riding her horse below. It's as if he thinks he might eventually be able to touch her if he leans forward just a little more. I can see in the depths of his foggy eyes what he imagines about her: how her life is a fated, unending, cruel prison, where she is driven forever by the crack of the ringmaster's whip and forced to perform incredible leaps at the harsh bark of his commands. Now he seizes up as he watches her perform a handstand on the back of her horse and then, after she flips back into her saddle safely, he shakes a little. I recognize his fear and worry. He wants to go down to her. He wants to shout, "Stop this madness," and rescue her from what he perceives to be an exhibition of torture.

She performs one last leap through a hoop then, lands with utter perfection, smiling ecstatically, then is handed down by the ringmaster, who kisses her cheeks before lifting her hand with his into the air, giving her away to the audience like a bride. Beside me, the clapping roars in the spectator's ears once more, burning out any possibility of his desire to rescue her. She belongs to the audience forever.

He lays his head on the balcony railing as the girl leads her horse through the flaps of a dark exit, and then he begins to weep without realizing he's weeping.

I understand his torment. I've felt as much in the months I've spent coming here, being a spectator like him. I've put myself through a different kind of leaping and landing, all of it in the confines of my own mind, in my memories of Peter. In the end, though, it's a futile, self-defeating effort. You either act or are acted upon. I know this now, and I try to tell myself that it's not too late to change things.

But what place is there in Kafka's circus for a spectator to do anything but observe, to do anything but imagine yourself doing something, *anything*, but sit through the acts, watching from high up in the gallery?

❧

THE FIRST TIME I CAME to see Peter perform in Kafka's Circus was after my father sentenced me to death by drowning. That was a year ago. Before then, I'd been stifling myself in the bank, conscientiously checking figures, tabulating, penning my signature on papers, then handing them off to the next person who would take them to the next person, until they reached whatever vault awaited them for filing. Wherever those rooms were, I'd never seen them.

But that day, I'd grown so frustrated by that existence that when I came home, I made the kind of mistake I'd learned to avoid with father years ago. Closing the door behind me, I heard his bed in the nearby room creak as he rose, and then he began coughing as he entered the room where I was hanging up my hat and coat. As usual, he asked how my day was. Ordinarily I'd reply by telling him it had passed as always—nothing special—but that day, without thinking, I said, "It is an awful life I lead there. It would be better if I were dead, really."

At that, Father immediately stopped coughing, and his eyes grew wide with a familiar anger that struck like a match.

"You," he said. Just that. *You.* Then, as I realized my mistake and began to sputter an apology, he raised his hands in the air, forming them into fists, and began to shout.

"You ingrate," he said. "You imbecile. You good for nothing. You should be so lucky to have that job. You should be so lucky to live in these rooms, and to have that suit and that hat." Here he pointed to the hat and coatrack in the corner and slammed his fists into them, knocking them to the ground as though they were my own body.

His voice continued to grow louder as he bellowed incoherent curses, and as his voice grew, Father's body seemed to grow with it. Suddenly he was no longer the decrepit old man who lay in bed all day coughing and ordering me about after I'd come home from work. He was a giant now, filled up with rage, and as usual I was his target.

"You killed her, you know. It's your fault your mother died. It was *you* who did it. You broke her heart. So strange! So useless! By God, I wish she had never admitted you into this world!"

I clapped my hands over my ears and told him to stop, to please forgive me, but it was too late. He could not be quieted. His rage would have to seek its own end now. And I knew it would be a far worse end than any judgement he had cast upon me in the past.

"I condemn you," he shouted, waving his fists in the air like a wizard, "to death by drowning!"

His words held power over me, as they always had. And as always, I felt my body seize up, prepared to conform to his orders. Even though I screamed internally and told myself to not heed his curse, my body had a separate life of its own. Suddenly I had picked up my coat and hat, shrugged my flesh back into them, and was opening the door and running down the cobbled street I'd just come home by.

My legs carried me at a fast pace down several other streets, until I arrived at a bridge spanning a nearby river. Below me, the water swept by, faster than the cars crossing above. My hands clasped hold of the railing, and my legs began to climb over—first one, then the other—to bring me to the fate Father had pronounced in my judgement.

Oh, Mother, I thought, as I tried to fight my body, which always complied with Father's commands. She'd been the only thing to keep Father from hurting me when I was little. She'd been my protector. And when she died, life had been like this ever after.

Father was right about one thing, though. I was lucky, I understood in retrospect, to have that soul-deadening job at the bank. Being there at least provided me with an excuse to not endure his presence for a good part of the day.

I was hanging from the railing now, my legs dangling over the water rushing beneath me, still trying to force my body to not accept this condemnation. My knuckles turned white as I gripped the railing. And then, as I craned my head to peer below, instead of water flowing by, I saw the net beneath Peter's trapeze in his neighborhood. The net we'd fall into together after swinging together as boys.

A moment later, the vision disappeared. The water returned, but it was as though Peter and his net had saved me. Father's judgment was no longer in my ears, surging, compelling me to murder myself in the river. My mind was free of him again, and I could only think of bouncing in that net alongside Peter.

I pulled myself up seconds later, took a few deep breaths, then hastily set off to the rail station, buying a ticket to the town where I knew Kafka's Circus was performing.

THOSE FIRST FEW TRIPS I took to Kafka's circus, I was so green that someone who worked there must have reported me. Because as I stumbled through the exhibits and past carnival barkers, looking, I assume, frightened and determined all at once, I was eventually approached by the manager.

"You're looking lost, young man," he said. "How can I help?"

I was uncertain at first how to answer and had not yet learned the trick of withholding the truth from those who may not have your best interest at heart. I blame Father for that streak of self-defeating conformity. So, when I answered, I said, "I've come to see Peter, the trapeze artist."

The manager of Kafka's circus is a big barrel-shaped man with a long, drooping mustache. He does not seem so bad, really, when you get to know him a little. He's paid to organize people, and organize he does.

But he also seems to have a large heart for his performers, as well as a good word for all attendees who pass the tests and become a part of the circus themselves, as audience members.

"The trapeze artist," he said, grinning, slipping a silver flask out of his coat to offer me a nip of whiskey. I took a swig of his offering, then returned the flask. "He's the finest trapeze artist we've ever had at Kafka's Circus," said the manager. "I applaud you for your good taste. Here, let me show you to him then."

He took me to the big top, where we took seats side by side high up in the gallery. Then, out of the darkness swarming before us, a spotlight suddenly appeared, and bottled within that light was Peter, standing on the trapeze platform, bar in hand. A snare drum played somewhere in the shadows, and after the drummer reached his final beat, Peter swung through the air.

We seemed to sit there for hours, watching him, although it couldn't have been more than a performance of twenty minutes. Afterward, the manager walked me back down the steps and out to the gray light of the fading day to see me off. At the gates, he turned to ask me if I might have any talents of my own the circus might employ. He said this as though it were a compliment, and I assume in his mind, it was.

"No talent," I said, "but for watching, unfortunately."

To which the manager replied, "And no talent for watching anything but the trapeze artist at that, I've noticed!"

At first, I shrank from this observation. But, of course, it was true. If anyone took a moment to observe me with the same intensity I observed Peter, they could see what I was here for.

"He used to have only one trapeze," the manager said, opening his coat to retrieve his flask, offering me another swig before parting ways. "But listen to this: one day, while we're moving to a new location, the trapeze artist calls to me from atop the luggage racks and asks very sweetly if he can have another bar to swing on. He sounds to me like he might cry. So I tell him, *Of course you can have another bar, you fool. It would enhance the act, actually*. And I tell him that he shouldn't worry. But even after trying to appease him, the trapeze artist begins to cry and I have to climb up to him, all the way up there on top of a tall stack of crates and luggage, where I find the poor thing with tears streaming down his face. *Only the one bar in my hands,* he cries out, *how can I go on!*"

I blinked tears away myself, hearing this.

"Well," said the manager, "finally he quiets down and falls asleep, leaving me to watch him carefully through the rest of the evening. He's too good for me to let him hurt himself somehow. It was later that night, though, while he was asleep, that I saw the first signs of sorrow begin to etch themselves upon his brow. They appeared suddenly, like an invisible script some sorcerer had waved his hands over and brought to light. And ever since that day I've worried that we'll eventually lose him."

The second bar was eventually supplied, of course, which seemed to satisfy the trapeze artist to some extent, the manager said. "And to be honest, he did look happier being able to add variety to his performance, to attempt new feats. But I also saw something in him that still hesitated. He would swing and swing, he would tumble and twirl, and though the audience below roared for him, his face always remained grim."

"Terrible," I said, shaking my head.

"Until one day," the manager said, "I began to notice him tilt his head mid-tumble to look out at something in the distance. Then his hands clamped down on the bar, and I saw the briefest of grins rise on his face."

"What was it, if it wasn't the second bar that made him happy?" I asked.

"That day," the manager said, "was today, actually. That something was you, I think."

"I should go to him," I said then, looking around for whatever path would lead me to him.

"No, no," the manager said, calmly patting my arm. "You mustn't disturb him. He is a part of Kafka's Circus now. You are welcome, of course, to sit and watch him. You do have the makings of an audience member, after all."

❦

AN AUDIENCE MEMBER. I DIDN'T know what the manager had meant by that back then. I didn't realize it was a sort of invitation to join Kafka's Circus in my own way, in a particular role. To be an audience member. To watch. To always watch. And since that day, I've spent so many hours watching. I've lived through so many days of awful gazing. Unable to act. Believing I could not disrupt Peter's life here. Being unable to disrupt my own life, really, as after watching Peter at Kafka's Circus I would, as always, return home to live within Father's smoldering anger, which caused he and I to both choke and cough each day of our lives, as though we were constantly breathing in smoke. The bank still held me, too, as though the bank itself was one large vault, and I just another file housed within it.

The last time I traveled to the circus, the manager saw me and took me aside for one of his chats, which I realized too late was nothing more than a spell, like the sort Father could cast. But whereas Father laid curses, the manager cast charms. The manager hypnotized and calmed. He managed.

Peter never left his trapeze, the manager told me during that visit, except for those times when the circus pulled up stakes to travel, and even then he'd sit atop the stacks of their suitcases and boxes, perched above everyone. And as soon as the circus reconstituted itself on the outskirts of a new town, he'd scurry up to his platform once again, and would not come down for anything.

The manager had somehow subdued me with Peter's sorrow, I realized. Each time I'd visit, he'd place his hand upon my arm to reassure me he was taking care of Peter now, and despite Peter's sorrow, he'd make sure Peter continued being the star he was destined to be.

A bird in the cage of Kafka's Circus.

I had that thought this morning, after I'd already placed my signature on so many pieces of paper that would be filed away in places I've never seen and likely never will.

A bird in the cage of Kafka's Circus.

"No more," I whispered, lifting my head from my paperwork. And, afterward, the walls of my bank cell seemed to quiver.

I said it again, a little louder.

"No. More."

And after that, I rose from my desk and did not bother to tell anyone I was leaving.

❧

HALF AN HOUR LATER, ON the train to a town I've never visited before—where the circus has set up its dismal black and white tents surrounded by wrought iron fencing, as though it were a traveling graveyard—I began to curse myself for my utter susceptibility to the charms of a circus impresario, then tried to forgive myself a little. I told myself it was simply a weakness caused by growing up in the shadow of Father. Of course I would be easily tricked by a man with a friendly manner who offers me nips of whiskey like an old friend.

I cursed myself for watching, too, for watching everything pass before me and around me, like I once watched the river rush beneath me as I dangled from a bridge.

But I am here now, I tell myself. I am here now.

From up in the gallery, I wait in the darkness of the big top, at an hour when it seems as though I am the only one there. And then, as usual, the spotlight appears, with Peter encased within it. He turns to me briefly, our gazes almost meeting in mid-air, and sees that I am there. My heart swells, as it always does in this particular moment of recognition. In each other's eyes, we understand each other. In each other's eyes, we see someone we can embrace without fear.

Beside me another spectator appears, weeping, as though Peter has already begun his act, which brings tears to the eyes of those who can appreciate his ability to tumble through the air like a star in the heavens. And as the spectator's tears sweep down his face, I wrench myself free of my fears to rise from the seat I'd claimed so many months ago high up in the gallery.

I cannot hesitate if I am to truly do this, if I'm to carry out the plan my desire has compelled me to make. So, before I can think another thought, I run down the stairs, past the audience members who look up at my passing figure with scornful curiosity, until I reach the center ring, and stumble into the light, no longer a spectator but a sudden disturbance that brings their steam-like automatic clapping at Peter's arrival to a halt. The ringmaster looks as shocked and disturbed as the audience members. His jaw drops. He's about to say something. But I shake my head, as though I am giving one of Father's orders, and his mouth closes once more. After that, I begin to climb the ladder opposite of Peter's platform.

As I climb, pulling myself up rung after rung, the audience begins to roar and clap once more, which surprises me, as I'd assumed they would turn on me, an audience member who does not know his station in life, an audience member who has the audacity to leave his seat and climb into the air above. All of this, they seem to think, is just another part of the act. They love it. They love *me*, it seems, which is such an odd feeling after never having felt that kind of recognition from anyone but my mother. And, of course, from Peter.

At the top I hoist myself over the platform and grab hold of the second bar that had only been installed after great complaint from Peter, who stands on the platform opposite holding onto his bar with an outstretched arm, watching me now, as I've watched him for these many, many months.

"Shall we?" I shout across the chasm between us, noticing that no net has been strung across the space below.

Peter grins, then nods, sending new courage through me, and in the next instant we both leap forward, swing toward one another, and meet in mid-air, where he tumbles away from his bar and lands alongside me, holding onto my bar now, his knuckles white beside mine, provoking the audience to roar even louder.

"It wasn't about it only being the one bar," I said as we swing through the air. "Was it?"

Peter shakes his head slightly. "No," he says, as we continue swinging.

"We should leave this place," I say, and a crease of worry appears on Peter's brow. The same crease the manager must have noticed on the night Peter first asked for something he desired, something so simple as another bar to swing from.

"But where would we go?" Peter asks, sweat now appearing on his brow. "I only know one thing," he whispers. "How to swing up here in the air."

"Then we shall swing," I say. "There are more bars to swing from than what we see in the darkness of this tent."

"Let us swing then," Peter agrees, nodding again, encouraged by my answer.

So, we do. We swing. We swing through the air, gathering the force of our gravity together, hurling ourselves from one side of the tent to the other, surrounded by the applause of the audience, which bolsters us even further, lifting us higher into the air.

Louder and louder, the applause grows, until finally it lifts us so high, we burst through the top of the tent like a pendulum broken away from its clockwork. And then we swing out into the open air above, reaching for the next bar, and the next, and the next, until that place of suffering is far behind us. And even after that, we continue to swing—the only thing we know how to do—as we move further out and into the world.

STORY
NOTES

THE CURE

There is a secret in this book. Embedded within the pages of the introduction to this collection is a short story called The Cure, which I wrote many years ago, circa 2001, when I'd first returned home to Youngstown, Ohio to pursue a master's degree in English. I'd started to publish short stories over the prior two years, and I was still experimenting—finding my voice, as they say—and finding out what that meant for me. Part of finding my voice was in exploring the voices of others, to see what had come before me, and how others had brought forth old stories in new guises themselves. This was a pleasurable and satisfying artistic impulse for me, and once I recognized that, instead of feeling the so-called "anxiety of influence" often mentioned among literary critics and writers, I instead embraced the "ecstasy of influence," as the writer Jonathan Lethem calls it. Out of that embrace, I gave myself assignments to begin learning how to pursue that mode in different ways.

The Cure was the result of one of those self-assignments, one in which I also gave myself the task to write a story under five hundred words in length, if possible. I started with one of my favorite fairy tales, Little Red Cap (or Little

Red Riding Hood, depending on who or which culture you ask), and then I went forth with establishing a different voice for this fairy tale, a personal voice, not like the distant tale teller of the originals. I tried to think about what the characters in that old tale might look like in a modern version where a young girl is being cautioned about a big bad wolf, someone who might do something awful to her or to her grandmother. I thought about how the wolf in the original tale swallows his prey, and I wanted to present an inversion of that aspect that still communicated his predatory nature, but in a different way.

Some readers have read this as a story about abortion. I think that's a perfectly valid reading, but I think it has other ways it can be read, too. While I was writing it, I distinctly remember feeling as though I was describing the feeling one gets when someone they have fallen in love with, who is actually a danger to them, takes over their entire life, both body and soul.

SISTER TWELVE: CONFESSIONS OF A PARTY MONSTER

This story came to me after I was invited to contribute a story to *Glitter & Mayhem*, an anthology of speculative fiction stories themed around the dance club and party circuit. For anyone reading this who knows me well, you'll know that this was totally my jam! In the early 2000s, I spent a lot of time in clubs, mostly gay clubs, but really any club where you could catch a good beat and where everyone was having a good time. These were spaces where I was able to explore who I was, where people felt free to be themselves, or even to invent a new self, if they wanted. Club life is a lot of things, and often it's portrayed for its seedier aspects, but clubs were a place where queer people could feel safe, where you could retreat from the harsher, colder treatment of the world, and where you could find people like yourself in person, rather than in the alienating and anonymous niches of the internet. So when this anthology invitation came along, I felt primed to write something for it, and the very first thought I had was to write about the Grimm's twelve dancing princesses, who had always captured my imagination as a child in the duality of their lived formal lives as royalty, and their nighttime capers in an underground world where they danced all night with strangers. I wanted to capture the feeling of what that fairy tale meant to me as someone growing up in a remote, conservative rural town, and the freer spaces I found later, after I left home for college and discovered places where I could dance all night with the most wonderful of strangers, some of whom later became members of my made family.

And when the story was chosen to lead off the contents of the anthology, I knew I had hit the right notes, and that—as they say in the club—I'd broken it down.

FOR THE APPLAUSE OF SHADOWS

This was a difficult story for me to write because it has some personal experience tied up into the warp and weft of its tale. The original story I set to work on with this adaptation was Poe's William Wilson, which is a short story about doppelgangers, if you choose to read it that simply. William Wilson, though, is also a story about a boarding school setting, where two boys share the same name, but where one is clearly from an upper crust society and one from a lower level. Despite the fact that they share a name, the well-to-do William Wilson can't abide the idea that someone shares his namesake, and some of his physical likeness as well, especially someone whom he sees as inferior to him in some way. In the course of the original story, he does away with his lesser double, who continues to haunt him and cause trouble for him in later stages of his life. In the original tale, William Wilson kills his double, who, once unmasked, reveals the same face as his killer, so the story remains in this land of psychodrama. For me, though, I had read it as a story of narcissism, of someone from an upper class being unwilling to share the same space and breath as someone who is like him in any way, especially when the likenesses are so obvious. So, my revision of this story was to tell the narrative from the point of view of the so-called double, and to instead make the original narrator of William Wilson the "Other William Wilson" with this flipped perspective. I then re-interpreted the events of the original story through this new lens, reframed as a tale of revenge from a victim of class hatred, and I also incorporated the mythic realm of Death, a place or plane that fascinated Poe himself to explain how my William Wilson, the so-called double of the original tale, was able to seek out his murderer despite being confined to the realm of shadows after his own murder.

In essence, the story can be read on that level of social class differences, but it's also a story about unrequited queer love. As I mentioned at the beginning of this note, I have a bit of personal experience tied up in the writing of this story. Often many queer people fall in love with someone who, despite wanting to be in a relationship with them, may reject them socially, or pretend as if they don't exist, especially if anyone in their social world begins to suspect the nature of their hidden relationship. Many years ago, when I was much younger, I found myself in a relationship of that sort, and I'm glad I made it out of that space of being disappeared by someone who claims to love you. So this is also a story that investigates the ways that narratives like that work in the lives of queer people. We shouldn't have to be anyone's secret. We shouldn't have to be condemned to receive applause—recognition—from shadows in an underground world. We should be able to receive love and accolades in the light of day.

Eat Me, Drink Me, Love Me

Christina Rosetti's poem, Goblin Market, is one that has always captured me since I first encountered it in my first year of college. It's a narrative poem, and tells what seems, at least initially, to be a fairly straightforward kind of fairy tale to its Victorian audience with a moral about what type of girl is good and what type isn't. A variety of interpretations surround the poem, some that discuss the potential same sex relationship between the sisters, others that contextualize the goblin market in the poem as a reference to the capitalist market that had erected itself in Victorian England, and yet others seek to interpret the goblin market as more of a metaphor for the opium dens and drug trade that existed in the underbelly of Victorian society. All of these interpretations are interesting, and probably all of them are valid in their own ways. One interpretation alone isn't required to hold the throne, although those who seek power will have you believe otherwise. No story should be so reduced to one perspective.

In my retelling of Rosetti's Goblin Market, I sought to do a number of things: first, to translate the poem out of verse and into prose narrative. This wasn't terribly difficult to do, since the poem was already oriented to narrative linearity over language or structural play. It did, of course, mean doing away with the rhyme scheme, in order to simply narrate in prose. I did, however, try to keep hold of key rhymes from the original, or to invent a few of my own.

Secondly, I wanted to add a kind of social dimension to the narrative. Rosetti's characters exist, like many characters in fairy tales do, almost outside of a recognizable social structure. In this case, the story was about two sisters, Laura and Lizzie, who lived alone. It's an unlikely situation in that time period, and with no mention of families or social order that they might belong to, and because Rosetti herself was what I'd call a soft rebel—someone who rebelled against many of the conservative restrictions of Victorian society, but without being terribly aggressive about it—it seemed as though some of these societal markers being absent from the narrative in the original poem were spaces I could fill in, to create a larger sense of the relationships between characters in the world that gave birth to this poem.

When it comes to interpreting the goblin market, as I've said, there are a lot of ways one can interpret that feature, but the way I chose for the purposes of this story, which depicts a same sex relationship oppressed by society's demands for heteronormativity, was for the goblin market to be a place, or a space, like the underground dance hall my Sister Twelve discovers in her tale, where social constrictions can be unbound, where the other, truer self can awaken or transform. The outcome of this story for Laura is a sad (yet familiar) one. But she, as the teller of the tale, has her eyes on changing the story for the younger generation she's in charge of, to hopefully make a better world for them to exist in. Changing the world starts with altering how the story of the world is told, which is also an idea that—particularly for this collection of revisionist tales—is quite proper.

THE TRAMPLING

I've always been fascinated by the story of Dr. Jekyll and Mr. Hyde. I first encountered it in an old film version, as a child, where the ghastly transformation of Dr. Jekyll into his monstrous counterpart, Mr. Hyde, felt like the transformation of Bruce Banner into the Incredible Hulk, of Marvel Comics. But later, as an adolescent, and then even later still in my twenties as a student of literature, I had come across many variations on this particular trope of transformation or alteration between a mild-mannered, upstanding citizen of "decent" society into a monster that preys on the weak. Not Bruce Banner's Hulk at all, really, since in that graphic narrative, Banner is a victim of experimentation gone awry, and most of the subtext of that narrative is one in which he takes vengeance on the military-industrial complex that created his dual persona. In Dr. Jekyll's case, he's an upstanding citizen of the upper classes in Victorian England, and his experiments are ones that enable him to go into the so-called "lower depths" of society, where he eats and drinks his fill in brothels, and kills those who get in his way, particularly the prostitutes he abuses, essentially becoming a narcissistic psychopath, which may well be what Robert Louis Stevenson was indicating many upstanding members of the upper class were, if given the right "potion" to drink that would release the inhibitions of the public filters (masks) they usually use to maintain a façade of stony calmness and elitism.

Not every retelling or adaptation needs to encompass the entirety of a text. For The Trampling, I wanted to focus on one incident in the original novel, *The Strange Case of Dr. Jekyll and Mr. Hyde*, which is part of the opening of that book, where we are immediately thrust into witnessing a small girl child running through the streets, who is trampled over by Mr. Hyde, who happens to be running from the police or from a mob he's possibly incited elsewhere in the area with his dastardly deeds. In his getaway, he tramples over the child and harms her badly. In the original, people rouse in the early hours as they hear the child's wailing and discover her leg has been badly broken. Various people in the group that comes to her aid begin to put two and two together about the nature of Mr. Hyde, who has been plaguing the streets of London for a while by then. What I wanted to do with this short story was to take that one moment, where the child is trampled and the people gather to help her, and to extend it into a meta-exploration of everything that comes afterward in the novel, thus recreating the entirety of the novel's narrative within the space of a short story. In this case, the story you've read in this collection isn't very different from the original, plot-wise, but the form and the delivery of it are. Sometimes an adaptation means changing the form of the story, not necessarily the essence it contains.

Along with that alteration of the form from novella or short novel into short story, I wanted to really underscore what the nature of the Jekyll and Hyde story really was about, at least for me: an upper-class gentleman, so to speak, who can get away with murder, literally, because of his class and wealth, and how it is those as vulnerable and powerless as a child who are his victims. Much blame is given to Mr. Hyde, his alter ego, but by now we must all know that division is false one, a Victorian self-defense to abdicate any responsibility of those from the upper classes for their misdeeds.

THE CREEPING WOMEN

The Yellow Wallpaper has always been a favorite story of mine, since I first read it as a teenager. I appreciated the description of what it feels like to slowly lose one's grip on reality that Charlotte Perkins Gilman was able to put into words so concisely, and I appreciated the many layers of public and private life that she addressed in the story, and how private life—which these days is something very different, as people publicize many of their days hour to hour, via social media—could also be a prison, at least for the oppressed, in Gilman's day.

One of the things I wanted to re-examine in my version of this story was the relationship among the women in the household. I remember rereading the story years ago and thinking, what are the housekeeper (the narrator's own sister-in-law, Jennie) and the nursemaid (Mary) doing and thinking while this poor woman is essentially being kept prisoner in that remote estate? How, as women, might they feel, and what might (at least one of) their stories look like? What would explain their going along? I chose to write from Jennie's perspective, since she's the husband's sister, and in many ways has to function as Jane's jailer whenever he is away.

When I started to think about how to go about addressing the complex weaving of gender and sexuality identity dynamics that I wanted to explore in this retelling, I asked myself, "What would Sarah Waters do?" And that's all I needed as my guiding light, really. I had never really read John, the narrator's husband, as considerate and confused so much as patronizing and possibly conniving. I do admit that he might have really been considerate and confused, that any man of his stature and learning in that society would think they were doing something good despite the vast evidence in front of them to the contrary. But my own experience with people who attempt to impose their beliefs or ideas onto another individual has made me a little suspicious of the motives of others. Since I was going to explore Jennie's role in relationship to her essential position to be Jane's "warden" whenever John is away, I also felt there might be some particular reason why Jennie would also be pressed into this service. In reading a variety of literature from the period, I found a lot of examples of women who were subjugated by their own family members, who had been tricked out of their own inheritances (which could have at least made them financially independent, regardless of their status in society) and I thought, yes, let's open up the edges of The Yellow Wallpaper and let some of these other kinds of gender dynamics and examples creep into the story, to open a wider view into that world.

INVISIBLE MEN

I first read *The Invisible Man*, by H.G. Wells, when I was fifteen or sixteen years old. Wells was new to me then, as most things are new to anyone at that age, and his science fiction novels enthralled me. In this particular novel, I enjoyed that the setting was largely a rural village despite there being a major scientific experiment happening and a fugitive hiding within its borders, in that most innocuous of places: the village inn. Having grown up in a small, rural town myself, I felt invited into that setting, even though it was in another country, and even though it was set in an unfamiliar period of time. I recognized many of the characters Wells wrote about, and some of his depictions of the pastoral setting in which he had set this mysterious and strange tale.

In my mid-thirties, I happened to chance across the 1933 film version of *The Invisible Man*, which made me interested in revisiting the novel. When I dipped back into the novel, though, I found it completely different than I had recalled it. Many of the qualities I enjoyed when I was a teen were still present, but I felt estranged from many of the characters that I had, in my memory, "recognized" as a young person. As an adult reader, the characters in *The Invisible Man* felt more like caricatures, and in particular the character of Millie, the young maid who works in the inn where the Invisible Man hides for several months as he tries to find a way to reverse his condition, felt as though she was being ill-treated, not just by her employer, but by Wells himself. In that later reading, she came across as a caricature of an ignorant village girl. Everyone in the novel tends to ridicule her, and Wells himself seems in many cases to agree by the tone he often takes about her. As an adult this kind of portraiture bothered me. I felt as though Wells was being classist in his depiction of most of the characters, and Millie especially took the brunt of that unjust portrayal. I began to imagine what life might be like for a young girl of fifteen or sixteen, whose life was already committed to living and working for the rest of her days in the employ of Mrs. Hall, who constantly demeans her. And soon I began to hear her voice speaking to me, trying to tell a different tale, one about herself from her own experience.

The difficulty with reaching across time and space is in trying to do it justice. So, to inform that voice I wanted to capture, I began studying some historical pieces from the setting of the book, and in my research, I came across *A Dictionary of the Sussex Dialect: A Collection of Provincialisms in Use in the County of Sussex*, by Rev. W.D. Parish. This was the absolute pot of gold at the end of the rainbow. A linguistic study from the same time and place that *The Invisible Man* was set, and I threw myself into the slang of that setting with great enthusiasm. I wanted to pick out pieces of language that the characters would have used, because the metaphors of the time and place were so rich, and the style of the language was so sassy and quick. Between the period study and the study of the local slang, I began to build out Millie's voice in a way that allowed me to access her and to, hopefully, re-create her as a fully dimensional character.

The story was originally published in the online magazine, *Eclipse*, edited by Jonathan Strahan, and later it was selected for reprint by Gardner Dozois for *The Year's Best Science Fiction*, an honor I had never thought I'd enjoy, as I don't really write science fiction so much as various kinds of fantasy. But the sort of science fiction that Wells wrote has the feeling of fantasy in many ways, so it wasn't too far astray from my impulses as a writer. I had always admired the editorial work of Gardner Dozois and was thrilled that something I'd written had captured his attention, enough for him to select it for his prestigious year's best anthology.

DOROTHY, RISING

All of the stories in this collection are obviously in conversation with their originating narratives. But there are also different kinds of conversations happening that are not as easily perceived at first glance. Dorothy, Rising is an example of one of those less easily perceived literary conversations, which I'll sprinkle some dust over here to reveal the invisible ink.

When I was writing this story, I was thinking about the aspects of social realism that is somewhat subdued in the text of *The Wizard of Oz*. The cultural conversation about that novel (and film) has been ongoing for decades, and because of that, we tend to have a lot of shorthand references, and whoever you're talking to will almost always know exactly what you mean.

For me, I wanted to focus on the first chapter of that novel, when Dorothy is transported by way of the tornado to Oz. I wanted to focus on highlighting the dismal poverty she comes from, and a kind of language that accompanies that landscape of despair that she escapes from during her time in Oz. I wondered about things that aren't asked as often: she's raised by an uncle and an aunt. What happened to her parents? Are her uncle and aunt blood relatives, or an adoptive foster family with whom she uses familial terms? The time period out of which L. Frank Baum wrote this story is a fairly bleak episode in American history. For readers in that time period, much of the cultural understanding of their contemporary circumstances would be immediate in how it informs this story. For current readers, maybe not so much. So, I decided to emphasize aspects of that historical social reality that provides the foundation of this story's setting.

I was also in conversation with another writer, though: not L. Frank Baum at all, but the writer Steven Millhauser, who wrote a story called Alice, Falling, that is a long, descriptive narrative about Alice, of *Alice in Wonderland*, falling through the rabbit hole. The story details that experience in such a way that, in Millhauser's hands, that moment from the original novel becomes its own story. In doing some research about *The Wizard of Oz*, I also discovered that L. Frank Baum was very taken with *Alice in Wonderland*, and that in many ways the transportation of the heroine, Alice, by way of falling through a rabbit hole, or tunnel, was deliberately inverted by Baum to transport his own young heroine by way of a tornado, its own kind of tunnel, or funnel, but pulling her upward instead. When I discovered that bit of influence Lewis Carroll's novel had on Baum, I started to triangulate with Millhauser's story about Alice falling through the rabbit hole, and created a parallel story for my Dorothy, rising up through the funnel cloud. I also wanted to chart the "rise" of Dorothy to Oz through that tornado with an aura of someone rising from the gray and dismal life she endures into a strange land of powerful magic users, con men, and massive wealth. A very American story, for sure.

THE BOY WHO GREW UP

I've always had a soft spot for the world of Peter Pan, which to me has always been this strange and personal mythology that goes beyond traditional fairy tale and into a completely open-bordered psychological fantasy tale. Like most people, I had encountered Peter Pan as a child through the popular play, and then later in various adaptations in film (my favorite of which is *Hook*, where we meet Peter Pan as a middle-aged man who has returned to the mortal world and grown up, though he's forgotten he's chosen to do that).

Later, though, in my mid to late twenties, I started digging into other Peter Pan texts, and discovered that J.M. Barrie himself, the originator, was in his own way constantly rewriting the story of Peter Pan. The first appearance of Peter was as an in-set story in a chapter of an adult novel Barrie wrote called *The Little White Bird*. That chapter became talked about by the novel's readers, and later Barrie published that chapter on its own as a children's book called *Peter Pan in Kensington Gardens*. After that came the play (which Barrie famously continued to rewrite from year to year between performances for quite some time until he settled on a final version). Then, after the play, Barrie wrote a novel called *Peter and Wendy*. Finding this breadcrumb trail of various iterations of Peter Pan from Barrie himself interested me, because so often when we think of retellings and adaptations, we assume that a modern author is adapting a tale from the past, rather than a writer potentially retelling or adapting a story they originated themselves.

For my entry into the world of Peter Pan, I wanted to write about the interplay between the cold, realistic world, and the fantasy land that Peter inhabits, so I created a teenaged narrator who is queer, working class, and dealing with a parent who's wounded him and their family in ways that have sent him seeking out sustenance from elsewhere. He stumbles upon Peter in this search and is introduced to some of the features of that original depiction of Peter in *Peter Pan in Kensington Gardens*.

That original iteration of Peter Pan is quite darker than the children's play, the novel that came after, or most of the adaptations I've come across. In it, Barrie makes it clear that Peter Pan is not "the boy who wouldn't grow up" simply because he didn't want to deal with the world of adults. Peter is "the boy who wouldn't grow up" because he has already died prior to the incarnation in which you, the reader, are meeting him in the story, and because of that a grave irony hangs over Peter's forever-child existence.

Barrie himself had a brother who died in his youth, and whose death colored the life of their family ever after. For Barrie, Peter became a metaphor for that child, his brother, who would never grow up, who was an eternal child because his life had ended in childhood.

I wanted to restore some of those unnerving and grimmer aspects of Peter's origin story through my tale. Often readers who haven't encountered this particular origin story, or some of the bits and pieces of J.M. Barrie's own life that I've relayed here, tend to think of Peter Pan as one of the purest vessels of childhood innocence and adventure they've ever encountered. For those who do eventually encounter this origin story, though, many come away, like the narrator of my retelling, feeling at least a little unsettled by their encounter with that both prime and primal version of Peter.

THE 24 HOUR BROTHER

Of all the stories in this collection, this one might be the one that lands furthest afield from its original narrative, The Curious Case of Benjamin Button, by F. Scott Fitzgerald. I had initially come across that story primarily because a film adaptation of it was released in 2008, which dramatized the life of a person who was born elderly and aged backwards. This was a real oddball idea, I thought, and when I learned that it had been drawn from a short story by F. Scott Fitzgerald, I was surprised. Fitzgerald is known for his realist depictions of the upper classes. I would never have guessed he'd even dabbled occasionally with fantasy concepts. So I became curious about "The Curious Case of Benjamin Button" and looked it up to give it a read.

I was not excited by the execution of Fitzgerald's story, which felt more like caricature than the portraiture he's known for, but I did still find myself thinking about the story and its concept for a long time after. This is usually a sign that something in a story has either resonated with me or has bothered me. In this case, it was the latter. I couldn't get on board with the idea of aging backwards. It didn't feel like the metaphor connected to how life happens or feels. I was happy to entertain the idea, but in the end the story made me think about how life felt much more the opposite of what Fitzgerald had depicted: that we move through life at such a fast pace, and seemingly ever-quickening as we age, that before we realize it, life has proverbially passed by in a blink of the eye, and what we retain are bits and pieces of memory, which we try to collect to bring a sense of understanding and purpose to our lifetimes, and what meaning we want them to hold.

So, while this story doesn't dig around in the literal aspects of the Fitzgerald narrative (I don't use the characters, setting, or plot), it does deal directly with the concept Fitzgerald explored, which didn't sit right with me. I turned the direction of the story and its premise around, then reset it to play out in a way that describes what being alive and time passing feels like, at least in my view of things.

Later, I discovered the writer Andrew Sean Greer had published a novelistic adaptation of the Fitzgerald story, *The Confessions of Max Tivoli*, which I thought was beautiful, and he rendered Fitzgerald's original idea in a way that made me truly fall in love with it.

KAFKA'S CIRCUS

Of the retellings and revisions and adaptations collected in this book, this one is perhaps the closest to my heart, if that is possible, since the originator of its material is Franz Kafka, a writer who is known more for his cerebral impulses and narrative effects. But despite Kafka's fiction often being viewed as intellectual explorations of the absurdity of life, I always found a human heartbeat in his stories of sons whose patriarchal fathers debase and demean them, sons who would throw themselves off a bridge into the rushing waters of a river below if their father declared that he must do so, sons who wake up transformed into a monstrously large insect. Or, in other stories: the exhaustion of an artist who starves himself for the entertainment and pleasure of others, a mouse who sings but whose community does not appreciate her rare talent, or trapeze artists whose happiness is only possible while they're swinging through the air.

This was also the most difficult of the stories in this collection for me to write. Largely because it does not correspond with one story directly, but with several stories of Kafka's, so the adaptation is one that has a more complicated construction.

I had identified a variety of Kafka's stories that presented characters who all were, in the end, either sideshow freaks or circus performers, like some of those characters I've mentioned above. There is The Hunger Artist, and the woman who rides on horseback in a big top performance in the story fragment called Up in the Gallery; and then there is the trapeze artist from the story called First Sorrow. Along with those figures is a mouse who sings in the story, Josephine the Singer, or the Mouse People. Josephine originally had an appearance in this story, but I cut her from it in the end, because I didn't feel her character made sense to a reader who would perhaps classify her as an anomaly among human artists in a circus or sideshow world. I wanted to create a story that could unite many of these carnivalesque characters into one setting, and for that I needed to find a conflict that could bring them all together. To do that, I turned to yet another Kafka story, The Judgement, where the conflict is one that powers many of Kafka's stories, where a son lives a life of abject torment, and whose tormentor is his father, who does not understand, appreciate, or even particularly like his son in general. Patriarchs tend to be unable to find meaning in anything but the most practical yet stultifyingly boring aspects of survival in this existence, and their families and children often suffer the brunt of that disposition.

The conflict at the heart of this story comes from that common Kafka story, and the setting and personages that act out that conflict in this case are the ones from Kafka's sideshow and circus characters. It was a long and winding road I had to travel to find my way to the story you've read in this collection, but the journey there was, for me, the kind of challenge that made me happy to keep coming back to figure out how to get to the destination.

In the end, all of the stories in this collection brought me that same kind of delight and satisfaction in discovering how to write them. The narrative of the artist as originator of something wholly new is a bit of a myth, really, and has caused anxiety for many who haven't wanted their influences to be so apparent. For me, wearing these influences on my sleeve, embracing them, reanimating them, restoring them, refashioning them, made the process of writing a story something new and transformative. Teaching myself how to alter art, in the end, altered me as an artist.

FURTHER READING

As I wrote these stories, I sought out adaptive and revisionist writing by other authors to study their work in this tradition. What follows is a list for those also interested in adaptive and revisionist writing.

Song of Achilles, by Madeline Miller

Mary Reilly, by Valerie Martin

Grendel, by John Gardner

Mr. Fox, by Helen Oyeyemi

Wide Sargasso Sea, by Jean Rhys

Transformations, by Anne Sexton

The Bloody Chamber, by Angela Carter

On Beauty, by Zadie Smith

Memoirs of Elizabeth Frankenstein, by Theodore Roszak

Going Bovine, by Libba Bray

Bridget Jones's Diary, by Helen Fielding

The Jane Austen Book Club, by Karen Joy Fowler

Ulysses, by James Joyce

Wicked, by Gregory McGuire

Snow White, by Donald Barthelme

Kissing the Witch, by Emma Donaghue

Lavinia, by Ursula K. Le Guin

Rosencrantz and Guildenstern Are Dead, by Tom Stoppard

PUBLICATION HISTORY

The Cure originally appeared in The Vestal Review, 2002

Sister Twelve: Confessions of a Party Monster originally appeared in
Glitter and Mayhem, 2013

For the Applause of Shadows originally appeared in
Where Thy Dark Eye Glances, 2013

Eat Me, Drink Me, Love Me originally appeared in
Once Upon a Time: New Fairy Tales, 2013

The Trampling originally appeared in Nightmare Magazine, 2015

The Creeping Women originally appeared in Uncanny, 2016

Invisible Men originally appeared in Eclipse Online, 2012

Dorothy, Rising originally appeared in The Fairy Tale Review, 2014

The Boy Who Grew Up originally appeared in Uncanny, 2014

The 24 Hour Brother originally appeared in Apex Magazine, 2011

Kafka's Circus is original to this collection

ACKNOWLEDGEMENTS

I would like to thank first and foremost my publisher at Lethe Press, Steve Berman, for bringing this collection of stories into the world. I would also like to thank the individual editors of magazines and anthologies that gave space to some of these stories in their first publications: John Klima, Lynne Thomas, Michael Thomas, Paula Guran, John Joseph Adams, Jonathan Strahan, Kate Bernheimer, and Mark Budman. I'd also like to thank Gardner Dozois for including "Invisible Men" as one of his selections to reprint for his esteemed anthology, *The Year's Best Science Fiction*. Without them, these stories would not have found their first audiences.

I would also like to thank my friend, the writer, Richard Bowes, who served as a constant sounding board for me as I wrote many of these stories. Without his knowledge and perspective, so much of my life would be different now, both as a writer and as a person in general.

Thank you, too, to Barry Goldblatt, for his unflagging belief and support.

Thank you to Matt Cheney, too, for his constant friendship and support over the years. It means more than I can say.

Thank you, too, to Mary Rickert, Sofia Samatar, Christopher Rowe, Gwenda Bond, Anya DeNiro, Kristin Livdahl, Kelly Link, Gavin Grant, Karen Fowler, Molly Gloss, Ted Chiang, Richard Butner, and Barb Gilly, whose friendship and missives span years, even in the ones when I've been in a cocoon, quietly becoming again.

And thank you to all those friends and family whose mere presences in my life help me to keep moving, and to keep telling stories.

ABOUT THE AUTHOR

Christopher Barzak is the author of the Crawford Fantasy Award winning novel, *One for Sorrow*, which has been made into the Sundance feature film *Jamie Marks is Dead*. His second novel, *The Love We Share Without Knowing*, was a finalist for the Nebula Award and the James Tiptree Jr. Award. His third novel, *Wonders of the Invisible World*, received the Stonewall Honor Award from the American Library Association and most recently was selected for inclusion on the Human Rights Campaign's list of books for libraries in LGBTQ welcoming schools. He is also the author of two short story collections: *Birds and Birthdays*, a collection of surrealist fantasy stories, and *Before and Afterlives*, a collection of supernatural fantasies, which won Best Collection in the 2013 Shirley Jackson Awards. His most recent novel, *The Gone Away Place*, received the inaugural Whippoorwill Award, and was selected for the Choose to Read Ohio program by the State Library of Ohio, the Ohioana Library Association, and the Ohio Center for the Book.

Christopher grew up in rural Kinsman, Ohio, has lived in the southern California beach town of Carlsbad, the capital of Michigan, and has taught English outside of Tokyo, Japan, where he lived for two years. He currently teaches creative writing at Youngstown State University.

Printed in the USA
CPSIA information can be obtained
at www.ICGtesting.com
LVHW090554050124
768064LV00005B/476

9 781590 217610